BORN

A COLORED

GIRL

BORN

A COLORED

GIRL

MICHAEL EDWIN Q.

Born A Colored Girl by Michael Edwin Q.
Copyright © 2018 by Michael Edwin Q.
All Rights Reserved.
ISBN: 978-1-59755-478-7

Published by: ADVANTAGE BOOKS™
                  Longwood, Florida, USA
                  www.advbookstore.com

Library of Congress Catalog Number: 2018941924

1. Fiction:: African American - Woman
2. Fiction: African American – Historical
3. Social Science - Slavery

Cover Design: Alexander von Ness

First Printing: April 2018
18 19 20 21 22 23 24   10 9 8 7 6 5 4 3 2 1
Printed in the United States of America

Life is made up of desperate hours.
In between, we find moments of joy.
A mother and daughter separated so long ago
Are about to be reunited.
They will reach out to each other
Across miles, time, and even across the grave.
From her mother's diary,
Etta Jean will learn to love the mother she never knew.
And from that same diary,
A mother will finally give of herself.

Chapter I

After All These Years

The bond between mother and daughter is strong, close, and for life. It is nearer than sisters, sweeter than honey, and eternal. To Etta Jean, such statements felt neither true nor false, fact nor fiction, being separated from her mother at an early age. All she remembered was that she was born to a young slave girl, which made her a slave as well, at least for the early years of her life. She knew she once had a father named Richard whom she held even fewer memories of and that she was one of four children whose names she no longer remembered. She had been separated from her family at the age of four.

Through a series of events that some folks would call a streak of good luck – and others, nothing short of a miracle – Etta Jean did not remain a slave for long.

Though free for most of her life, she understood the limitations that society placed on her with her ambitions always exceeding her grasp. Every city she lived in had a designated area for *her kind*. Only certain people and opportunities were available to her.

She was raised in foster homes provided by church people who could afford to take her in for only so long. She bounced from home to home. By her mid-teens, she had blossomed into a tall and slender beauty. Many of the young men of the congregation had an eye for her, but she held onto other dreams.

At seventeen, with her few belonging in a suitcase, she left her small Southern town and headed north to Boston to seek a better life.

In Boston, in the black part of town, with what little money she had, she rented a small room in a boarding house run by the Widow Faye Wilkins. It was a large three-story Victorian home broken up into single rooms which the Widow Wilkins mostly rented out to men working the factories in the city. Most of her guests were married men who sent money home every week back to their families in small Southern towns, each of them planning and hopping to someday save enough money to get a small place in town and send for their families.

The Widow Wilkins was a short, stout, middle-aged lady of fine manners and sharp business sense. She carried herself with great dignity. She always dressed in elegant clothing, and her manner was one of self-pride. Her hair was just turning gray on the sides. She was an admirable figure of a woman, and though she had seen better days, she could still turn a head or two. Most of the time she went about with a fun-loving attitude, but she could turn it off as quick as an oil lamp when need be. In business, she was a no-nonsense woman.

Little did Etta Jean realize that the Widow Wilkins and the boarding house would play a major role in her life. Etta Jean was the only female guest of the boarding house. Being young and innocent, Mrs. Wilkins took her under her wing. The widow, having a motherly nature, and Etta Jean, growing up motherless and never knowing much about her true mother – the two hit it off well from the start. Knowing Etta Jean's plight, and having recently lost one of the help at the boarding house, Mrs. Wilkins offered Etta Jean a job with a fair wage that included bed and board.

The job consisted of many different tasks to make for a busy day, up early in the morning, to kitchen work, cleaning rooms, and then laundry.

Each day, she would have a few hours alone in her room; usually she'd read a book or her Bible.

They served no lunch at the boarding house, except on Sundays. The rest of the day she spent cleaning, dusting, and doing laundry. At midday, she returned to the kitchen to prepare the evening supper, which they served promptly at five thirty. The rest of her evening was her own, again mostly spent in her room reading or socializing with Mrs. Wilkins in the parlor with some of the guests.

Under the Widow Wilkins' guidance, Etta Jean's job became more than a way to make a living; it was an education. She learned how to do chores in quantity, but best of all, she learned to have a good head for business and to manage her money wisely.

She worked seven days a week with every other Sunday off. The Sundays she did work, they started late so the staff could go to church. Mrs. Wilkins saw to it Etta Jean attended and became an active member of a good local church. It was at this church that again Etta Jean's life took another turn for the better.

After a few months, Etta Jean enjoyed the repetition and security of her life. And one Sunday afternoon at a church picnic, she met Thomas Newman.

Thomas was a tall, slender, handsome, young black man. His arms were strong and wide from work. His chin came to a sharp point and gave nobleness to his looks. There were many women in the congregation who secretly yearned to know him. Though the pastor's wife often went out of her way to introduce him to some of the eligible women in the congregation, his head was never turned. Thomas possessed a strong spiritual life and was deeply involved in the church. He led a men's Bible study on Wednesday nights and was seldom seen without the Good Book far from his side. Though he was well-educated, his education did him little good. He was a laborer at one of the factories like all the other young men in the parish. But his high intelligence did help make him shine, and he was promoted to floor manager, overseeing quality control – only over the black workers, of course.

Thomas lived at a different boarding house three blocks from Mrs. Wilkins'. He wasn't a drinker or a gambler. He was a bit of loner and kept pretty much to himself. But this all changed when he was introduced to Etta Jean, and only a few weeks later they were courting. It went on for nearly a year. Their relationship grew deep and strong. Neither one of them could ever remember if he ever really did propose marriage to her; it just seemed the natural thing to do.

It was a June church wedding. Mrs. Wilkins was the matron of honor. They held the reception in the church hall filled with the smiling faces of co-workers and friends. It was a potluck dinner with plenty for all. The adults stood talking and laughing for hours as children ran through the crowd chasing one another.

The loving couple slipped away silently when no one was looking and the hour was late. Etta Jean suspected they would go to Thomas' room. But to her surprise and delight, he took her two blocks north. They stood before a two-story brownstone. Etta Jean looked at him in bewilderment.

"This is your new home," he said proudly. "It's all ours ... that is, after thirty years of payments it will be."

He'd put down nearly all of his savings. Etta Jean wrapped her arms around his neck and kissed him. When Thomas carried her over the threshold, it was the first time in her life that she felt that she was finally home.

* * * * * * * *

Etta Jean continued working for Mrs. Wilkins, and Thomas worked long and hard hours at the factory. They made a good life for themselves, and it was clear to everyone how much in love and happy they were. But sometimes when you think things couldn't get better, they do. What they shared was nothing compared to the joy they felt when they learned Etta Jean was with child. Early the next year, the child was born and she was beautiful. Over much discussion, they decided to name her Liberty.

The next few years were full and fruitful. But sometimes life takes an about-face and things go bad – sometimes heartbreakingly bad.

They didn't even have the decency to tell Etta Jean face-to-face. They sent a small boy, little George who swept the floors and cleaned out the bins. When Etta Jean opened the front door, the poor child stood there quivering with fear.

"Mrs. Newman, this here's for you," he said, handing her an envelope and running away in fear as if the devil was after him. Before she could say anything, little George was gone.

Fearing the worst, Etta Jean sat down in the parlor. Baby Liberty slept quietly in her bassinet. Etta Jean opened the letter. It bore the letterhead of the company Thomas worked for.

> *Dear Mrs. Thomas,*
>
> *It is with a heavy heart we regret to inform you that your husband, Thomas, met with a fatal accident on the job this morning.*
>
> *There is no reason to go into graphic detail. But we can tell you his passing was quick and painless. The factory doctor proclaimed him dead the moment he examined him.*
>
> *We've taken the liberty of transferring the body to Calverton's funeral parlor. Have no concerns, we feel it is our duty to pay all expenses, as well as a burial plot and tombstone at Westland Cemetery. It is the least we can do.*
>
> *If you have any questions or are in need of anything, feel free to contact us.*
>
> *When you feel up to it, please come to our office. There are papers to be signed concerning back pay and insurance.*
>
> *Again, feel free to reach out if you need anything.*
>
> *Our condolences in your time of grief,*
>
> *Walter Sternward*

Not only did they not have the decency to confront her, they had the gall to make all the arrangements without her. Paying for it would take the financial burden off her, but not even consulting her was a slap in the face. She would have been angry if not for the flood of sorrow that swept over her.

As if in solidarity, Baby Liberty burst into a fit of crying. Etta Jean took her up in her arms. She stood by the window gently bouncing the baby in her arms.

"It's okay, Liberty. Momma's here. Everything's going to be all right."

Inwardly, she knew she was lying to her daughter and herself. There was no way she could admittedly say that everything was going to be all right.

Once the child stopped crying and fell asleep, she placed Liberty back in her crib. The tears fell from Etta Jean's eyes. She looked out the window. The world was a blur and as unclear as their future.

* * * * * * * *

The funeral was a solemn affair. Calverton's funeral home was elegant, with red velvet drapes, dark wooden walls, and an organist playing soft and low. Surely, Etta Jean could not have afforded Calverton, if it weren't for the company's money. It was a closed casket. This told her that the death of her husband had been a horrible one that had disfigured his body.

It was during the funeral that Etta Jean found out the truth. Some of Thomas' closer coworkers told her the full story. A large and heavy piece of machinery rested on a wooden plank. The old and dry wood cracked, causing the piece of machinery to fall upon Thomas. He was crushed and died instantly. The only saving grace she had was in knowing he didn't suffer.

Again, Westland Cemetery was far out of Etta Jean's financial grasp, if not for the company's money. It was an integrated cemetery to an extent. Whites were buried in the area on the front of the property; black graves were in the back forty separated by a tall metal fence.

At the cemetery, Mrs. Wilkins held little Liberty to allow Etta Jean time to grieve. Looking around, she saw many of Thomas's coworkers and folks from the church. Each of them gave their heartfelt sympathy, but she was so deep within herself that she heard none of it.

There was only one representative from the company, a short, round, little, bald, pasty-faced, white man dressed in a dark suit that looked like he'd slept in it for days. One thin, long clump of hair was combed over the top his globe-like head in a sad compensation for his baldness. It was clear by the expression on his face he did not want to be there. He moved like a man stepping around snakes. He approached Etta Jean and offered her his hand, which was as cold and numb as a dead fish. As soon as he gave the company's condolences, feeling he'd done his duty, he disappeared.

The pastor prayed over the grave. Again, the words fell on her empty ears. Only the sound of her tossing a rose down into the grave upon her husband's coffin did she hear. To her, the sound was as loud as cannon fire, and it startled her back into reality. And in reality, all she could do was cry.

Back home, guests filled the house. Members of the church covered the kitchen table with food and drink. Understandably, Etta Jean did not feel like eating.

Thankfully, Liberty fell fast asleep, and Etta Jean placed her in her crib.

Hours later, people gave their condolences and began leaving. Etta Jean was thankful for them, yet she was glad they were leaving. Only Mrs. Wilkins remained.

"Is there anything you need before I leave?" she asked Etta Jean.

Etta Jean sadly shook her head.

Mrs. Wilkins put her arms around her and hugged her. "If there's anything you need, you just ask. Don't worry about coming back to work. You take as much time as you need. I love you, child."

These words Etta Jean heard because they were heartfelt. She cried in Faye Wilkins' arms. In time, the two broke loose of each other and sorrowfully smiled into each other's eyes.

After Mrs. Wilkins left and the door closed, Etta Jean sat in the parlor alone. A strange feeling came over her. Being an orphan from an early age and moving from foster home to foster home until she set out on her own, Etta Jean believed she knew what being alone felt like. But this was something different. This was like being surrounded by walls of ice with the outside world miles away with no one to hear her scream, even if she did. This was the deepest and darkest place she ever imaged she'd ever be. If not for the love of her daughter, she might have given up and died.

* * * * * * *

A week after the funeral, Etta Jean placed Liberty into the care of Mrs. Wilkins for the day and went down to the office of the factory. Again, she was not met by anyone in upper management. But she was taken to the office of one of Thomas' managers. She was met with a handful of papers to sign.

She was faced with another lower manager who wanted to get the meeting over as soon as possible.

"What am I signing?" Etta Jean asked.

"It's just a formality," said the manager. "It's all of your husband's back pay, and there is an insurance settlement."

It would seem the company had a little scam going. The factory was a dangerous place to work so they insured all their workers. In case of death or dismemberment, the insurance company would pay up: sixty percent going to the company and forty percent to the family of the injured party.

Of course, it was scam. But what was one to do? It was better to agree to forty percent than nothing. And forty percent was better than a poke in the eye with a sharp stick. And besides, it would help with the mortgage payments. Perhaps, Liberty and she could remain in their home.

Etta Jean agreed to the terms. What else could she do? She was at their mercy, and there was no way to fight or disagree. A larger power than she made the rules. Etta Jean and her daughter sailed in a small ship on a large ocean, and the powers that be were ready to make large waves. She agreed to the terms and signed the papers.

* * * * * * * *

Etta Jean returned to work at Mrs. Wilkins' boarding house. Her wages would keep them in food and clothing. The insurance money would pay the mortgage and keep the wolf away from the door, but it would still be a struggle. The church had a program for children where Liberty spent her time while her mother worked. In time, she was old enough to attend public school. As progressive as Boston was, it was still a school for blacks only.

The years seemed to pass by both slowly and quickly, as time has a habit of doing. When Liberty turned nine years old, another unexpected turn happened.

It was a lazy Saturday evening. Liberty was studying her books, and Etta Jean busied herself with sewing that she did for extra money. Besides working for Mrs. Wilkins, she took in laundry and sewing, mostly for the elderly. Etta Jean worked constantly, except for when she was sleeping. And she would have worked in her sleep if she knew how. The life of a single mother is one of hard work and sacrifice.

There was a knock at the door. Liberty ran to see who it was. Standing in the doorway was a tall, handsome white man.

"You must be Liberty," said the man, smiling. "Is your mother home?"

Etta Jean walked up and stood behind her daughter. "May I help you?" she asked.

"Are you Mrs. Newman?" he asked.

It took a moment for Etta Jean to respond. Never in her life had she set eyes on such a well-dressed man, white or black, in her life. The Reverend Carter was the best dressed man she ever met, but this man outshined him. He wore a dark suit, waistcoat, and a heavy black coat. Clearly, what he wore was custom made for him, as everything fit perfectly. His black shoes reflected the surroundings like mirrors. A gold watch chain dangled from his waistcoat, and he wore two fine rings on his left hand, a wedding ring and a sapphire pinky ring. His fingernails were professionally manicured, and every blonde hair on his head sat uniformly as if he'd placed each strand there carefully one by one.

Finally, Etta Jean spoke, "Yes, I am. Can I help you?"

He took from his inner pocket a business card and handed it to her. "My name is Jaggers. I'm a lawyer from Colorado. I have a unique legal practice; I have only one client."

Etta Jean remained silent, waiting for Mr. Jaggers to finish.

"That one client is Elizabeth Walker ... your mother."

If he'd hit her with a two-by-four, it would have been a softer blow. She was speechless.

"I've come a long way, Mrs. Newman. May I please come in?"

"Yes, of course," she said, moving out of his way. "Liberty, why don't you take your books up to your room, please?" she said as Mr. Jaggers entered.

Liberty took her books and went upstairs while Etta Jean and Mr. Jaggers went into the parlor. She motioned for him to sit, which he did. She sat in a chair facing him, not saying a word.

"I realize this comes as a shock to you. First, let me say that your mother passed away a month ago. She died a very wealthy woman living in Colorado. Do you remember your mother, Mrs. Newman?"

"Not really."

"Well, she never forgot you. You're mentioned in her will."

"Mr. Jaggers, I don't want to be impolite, but my mother gave me up years ago, when I was a toddler. I've not heard a word from her in all those years. I'm sorry she died, but to be honest, I couldn't care less. The woman means nothing to me, as I'm sure I meant nothing to her. If the poor woman had regrets on her deathbed, it's nothing to me. Whatever she left me in her will, I want none of it. You can just give it all to some charity. Now, at the risk of sounding rude, could you please leave?"

A smile appeared on Mr. Jaggers' face. It was a gentle smile, but it seemed out of place on such a serious-looking man. "We figured as much – that is, your mother and I," he said. "Won't you give her a chance to explain?"

"And how would she go about doing that, since she's dead?"

Mr. Jaggers reached into his inner coat pocket and handed her an envelope. "Here's a letter of introduction from your mother. There are no answers in it, but perhaps you may find some here," he said as he reached into the deep side pocket of his coat and handed her a leather-bound notebook."

Etta Jean held both the envelope and the book. She opened the book. It wasn't in print; it was handwritten.

"The book is not in your mother's handwriting, but the letter is. When your mother learned she was dying, she wanted to get her story on paper. Each day, one of my secretaries visited her at her bedside and wrote down what she said. She died three days after its completion. She did it in hopes it might explain to you what happened and you would not judge her so harshly." Mr. Jaggers stood up. "I'll be staying at the Parker House if you need me. This is not the end of it. There is more to come."

"More...? What do you mean 'more'?" Etta Jean said, rising from her chair.

Mr. Jaggers walked to the front door and opened it. "Mrs. Newman, please, just read the letter and book. Perhaps then you'll understand. You know where to find me. If I don't hear from you, I'll be in touch."

He walked out, gently closing the door behind him.

Etta Jean was speechless. She didn't know what to think or do so she placed the letter and book down on the desk in the corner of the room. Then she walked to the bottom of the stairs and shouted up, "Liberty, dinner will be ready in a few minutes."

"I'll be right there, Momma," Liberty shouted down.

Etta Jean went to the kitchen to prepare dinner.

* * * * * * * *

After dinner, when Liberty was asleep in her room and the house was dark, Etta Jean sat in the parlor holding her mother's letter. She stared at it for the longest time before opening it. She knew everything was about to change, and change, though

necessary for life, is a frightening prospect.

Finally, she carefully opened the envelope. She unfolded the letter and leaned closer to the lamp to get a better look. It was only one page. The first thing she noticed was the handwriting. It was thin and shaky, the handwriting of someone very old or very sick.

Before reading a word, Etta Jean closed her eyes for a moment. She tried to remember what her mother looked like. But it was so long ago, and all she could picture in her mind is the silhouette of a woman hovering over her. She tried to remember anything her mother did for her, any interaction between the two of them. Not that it mattered really. This was the writing of a dying woman. This is not the woman she remembered, no matter how little memory there was. She opened her eyes. Holding the paper in her shaking hand, she read the letter.

My dearest child, Etta Jean,

I'm not sure I should be doing this, or what words I should say to you. Surly nothing I could offer can make it better. I'm sure you've been through much sorrow. For this I am sorry.

You are one of my four children. I doubt if you remember your brothers and sisters. There was Willy and Henry, your brothers, and Emma May, your twin sister. That's right. I don't know if you remember, but you had a twin sister. Do not bother to look for any of them. They can no longer be found in this world. Sadly, they've all passed on.

I tried for years to find them and you, but the war made it impossible. It wasn't till after the war that I made any headway. It broke my heart to learn all but one of you was gone. But my only glimmer of hope was when I learned you were alive and well. I wanted to rush to you when I learned of you, but the doctors say it's not to be.

If we had met, I know it would have been awkward. But we would have talked about our lives, the paths that led us to where we are now. I ache to know your story, but sadly I will never live to hear it. So I have put my life's story down on paper.

It is not a confession or a plea for forgiveness; I don't expect that. It is the only way I have of reaching out to you, reaching across so many years and miles, and now from across the grave. Please, read it. Perhaps after reading it, you won't judge me so harshly.

With all my heart,
Mother

Etta Jean was filled with mixed feelings. She sat in the dark, holding the letter till her eyes became heavy and she fell asleep.

Chapter II

She's Made It Possible

The next morning, Etta Jean woke early, still seated in the parlor chair holding the letter. It was Sunday. She woke Liberty to get ready for church while she prepared breakfast.

Sitting at the kitchen table, Liberty noticed something different about her mother.

"Are you all right, Momma?"

"I'm fine, dear. I accidentally fell asleep in the easy chair. Once I wash up and dress for church, I'll be right as rain."

"That's not what I mean," Liberty said. "Something's different about you."

It amazed Etta Jean how insightful her young daughter was. As much as she wanted to hide from her daughter, Liberty felt the change.

"We don't want to be late for church. Why don't you clear the table while Momma gets ready?"

Liberty nodded with a smile.

Walking through the parlor, Etta Jean took the letter and placed it in the notebook that still lay on the desk. She knew that life was about to change. For better or worse, she wasn't sure, but it was about to change. She rushed upstairs to get ready for church.

* * * * * * * *

During church, Etta Jean went through the motions. She raised her hands in praise, but her thoughts were a thousand miles away. She moved her lips but didn't sing the hymns; nothing came from her mouth but air. She sat staring into space, not listening to the preacher. All she could think about was the letter and how in less than a day her entire world had changed. She couldn't wait till after church when she could speak with Mrs. Wilkins.

"Would you like to come to the house for something to eat?" Etta Jean asked Mrs. Wilkins as they and the others shuffled out of church after service.

"I'd love to, darling, but we're serving ham for lunch. If I'm not there, they'll cut the slices too thick."

"Faye, I wish you'd come to the house, even for a short time. I've something I need to talk over with you."

Mrs. Wilkins saw the troubled look on Etta Jean's face. The mother in her rose to the surface.

"Oh, what the heck…let them cut as thick as they like."

With Liberty holding onto her mother's hand, the two women walked arm in arm to Etta Jean's home.

"Liberty, could you please go up to your room while I talk with Auntie Faye?" Etta Jean asked as she opened the front door.

"First give your Auntie Faye a hug," Mrs. Wilkins said before the child ran up the stairs.

The two women sat in the parlor.

"So what's troubling you? Mrs. Wilkins asked.

"You've always been so good to me and my little girl. I've always thought of you as my mother in many ways."

"So what motherly advice do you need?"

"A lawyer came to see me yesterday, my mother's lawyer."

A look of shock appeared on Mrs. Wilkins' face.

"It seems my mother died recently. She died a wealthy woman. She found out where I was just before she died and had her lawyer deliver a letter from her and a book of her memoirs."

Etta Jean walked to the desk and handed the letter to Mrs. Wilkins. She took her time reading.

"No wonder you're so upset," Mrs. Wilkins said.

Then Etta Jean handed her the notebook. Mrs. Wilkins thumbed through it.

"What should I do?" Etta Jean asked.

"There's nothing you can do but follow through. I know it's difficult, but you must read what your mother left you. It's the only link you have to her. Read it, and then make your decision."

Mrs. Wilkins walked to the front door. "I need to get going before they eat the entire ham. I'll see you in the morning."

Etta Jena looked confused.

"Don't let it worry you, dear. It's just life."

Mrs. Wilkins left, closing the door behind her.

* * * * * * *

The next morning after getting Liberty to school, Etta Jean went to work at the boarding house. It was like any other day. That is, till the end of the day. A young white man, slender and tall and dressed in an ill-fitting, inexpensive suit, arrived. His arms were too long for the sleeves, and there was a two-inch gap between the end of his pant legs and the tops of his shoes. He stood at the front door with his hat in his hand.

"May I help you?" Mrs. Wilkins asked.

"I have a message for a Mrs. Newman."

"Etta Jean, there's a man here to see you," Mrs. Wilkins hollered into the house.

Etta Jean came to the door. She felt worried. Lately, life was taking a side road, and she wondered what was coming next.

"Mrs. Newman, I'm supposed to see that you get this."

It was a business card. Before she could read it, the young man put his hat back on his head and tipped it politely. Then he turned quickly and was gone.

She read the card. It was the business card of Mr. Boise, the president at the bank that held the mortgage on her home. Etta Jean also had a savings account that couldn't have had more than one hundred dollars in it, and that had taken her years to accumulate. She turned the card over. On it was a handwritten message that read: "Please come to the bank as soon as soon as possible. We have important business to discuss."

A fear came over Etta Jean. A note to meet the president of the bank did not sound like any good would come of it. She thought hard: she couldn't remember being late on any payments. She'd kept good records of payments. But there were rumors of the law stepping over the line and accusing blacks of nonpayment. And in such circumstances, it was the banker's word against the accused, and the courts would only listen to words from certain mouths.

She arranged for someone to take care of Liberty and rushed down to the bank. It was past closing time. But when the guard saw her face in the window, he opened the front door and let her in.

"Mrs. Newman, Mr. Boise is in his office waiting for you."

When she entered, he closed and locked the door. She went to Mr. Boise's office and knocked on the door.

"Come in," said a voice from within.

Mr. Boise sat behind his desk. When he saw her, he stood up and smiled. He pointed to a chair in front of his desk. "Mrs. Newman, thank you for coming. Please sit down."

His smile and caring tone were not enough to convince her that all was well. It would not be the first time in her life that a sweet smile was accompanied with a stab in the back.

She sat down and began wringing her hands together.

"I don't know why I'm here, Mr. Boise. If I'm late on my mortgage payment, it couldn't be more than a few days. I promise I'll make it good."

"Your mortgage is the reason I've called you here," he said.

A chill shot up Etta Jean's spin.

"It seems someone has paid your mortgage off. You're paid in full."

Etta Jean was in shock. "'Paid in full'? I don't understand. Paid by whom?"

"A Mr. Jaggers from Colorado came by and paid the balance in cash. I have all the papers here for you to sign. I have your deed here as well."

Etta Jean was angry, happy, and confused. She signed the papers as if in a dream. Mr. Boise handed her the deed marked "paid in full," and then he walked her to the front door of the bank.

"This is truly your lucky day, Mrs. Newman. I'm very happy for you. I hope you take that money you normally pay against your mortgage each month and build up your account with us. When you have the time, I'd like to talk over some ways of investing. It's a pleasure doing business with you, Mrs. Newman. You have a wonderful day."

Etta Jean was surprised at Mr. Boise's tone. He'd always been very professional when dealing with her. But now he was more than friendly, he was showering her with accolades he'd never used before.

The next moment, in a dream-like state, she was out on the street, still holding the deed. Without another thought, she turned left and headed for the Parker House Hotel.

As for race relations, Boston was always a progressive city, before, during, and after the war. But there were still things that did not sit well with many Bostonians. One of them would be a black maidservant storming across the lobby of the Parker House Hotel. That's what backdoors were made for.

"I'm here to see one of your guests, a Mr. Jaggers," Etta Jean asked the gentleman behind the front desk.

The clerk looked at her inquisitively. To him, there was no reason for a black woman to visit a white guest. They had a cleaning service, so there was no need for a cleaning woman. As for another, more deviant reason, no self-respecting gentlemen would call for such a woman in the middle of day, nor would such a woman come straight through the front door. Again, that was what backdoors were for.

"Do you know what room Mr. Jaggers is in?" he asked, sounding very put off by her presence.

"No, I don't," she said calmly.

The clerk tapped the front desk bell three times. A young-looking bellhop appeared from nowhere.

"Tell Mr. Jaggers in room 419 there is someone in my office who wishes to speak with him."

The young man ran off toward the wide staircase.

"Now, if you'd please follow me, young lady?" the clerk asked. "You can wait for Mr. Jaggers in my office.

"I'm fine just where I am," Etta Jean responded.

He looked at her and shook his head.

"It's just that we don't want a scene," he said.

"There's not going to be a scene. I have some business with Mr. Jaggers."

"I'm afraid it's my office, or you'll have to leave," he said matter-of-factly, with an ice-cold stare.

"And if I refuse to do either?"

"Then I'll call the police. Make it easy on yourself and come to my office."

Etta Jean realized the uselessness of arguing her point. She followed the clerk to an empty office. Leaving her alone, he slammed the door. Etta Jean found a large leather couch off to one wall; she sat down and waited.

The next moment, the office door opened and in walked Jaggers wearing that smile he wore the other day, the one that didn't suit him.

"I suspected it would be you," he said.

"Of course, you knew it would be me," she said, standing and waving the deed in front of his nose. "What is this?"

"It's only one of many gifts and surprises from your mother."

"Well, I don't know if I like it," Etta Jean growled.

"You accepted it, didn't you?"

"Yes, I did. But there's something that doesn't feel right about it."

Jaggers' smile left his face, and he went somber.

"Of course, it doesn't. That's because it's a gift from someone you don't know, a stranger. Your mother is gone. You will never have a relationship with her in this world, at least not in the way you would hope for. But she's made it possible for you to know her. Go home. Take your time and read what she wrote. Get to know her. If after reading it, you still feel the same, I'll leave and you'll never see me or hear another word about your mother again."

The way he put it, it did not sound like an unreasonable request, though blunt and to the point.

"Very well, that's what I'll do."

"Good," he said. "I'll be here when you need me."

Mr. Jaggers held the door for Etta Jean. She walked past the disapproving clerk at the front desk and out of the hotel.

She collected Liberty on the way home. The evening was no different from any other night. They ate dinner; Liberty did her studies and then went up to bed. Etta Jean tucked her in and kissed her goodnight, and then she went back downstairs.

Alone, she picked up the book from the desk and sat in a chair close to the lamp. She took a deep breath and opened the notebook to page one.

Chapter III

Jealousy and Compassion

I was born a colored girl into slavery. That is what they called me, "the colored girl." To them it was a term of endearment, and it was, compared to the other names they sometimes called you, as you know. But it never sat well with me, being called colored. That implies that there is a group of people out there who have no color and that they are the normal ones. If that were true, then all the others are abnormal because they have been colored. But aren't all God's children colored? Some are white; some are black or brown, yellow, red or tan. All are colored.

Even as a young child, I knew instinctively that if I were to be considered as outside the realm of normality or to accept the notion myself, nothing good would come of me. So I fought the perception at every turn. In my life, this rebellious nature has been the source of much of my joys and most of my sorrows.

Ask me about my birth, and I couldn't tell you when or where, other than it was on a Southern plantation. Ask me about my parents, and you might as well ask me about Father Christmas. I don't know their names. Their faces are less than a blurred memory. I only remember them as vague images. Once I was weaned and able to move about and pick crops on my own, I was sold.

I came of age on the Walker Plantation in Virginia, thus the last name. I was one of many slaves. We worked the land and picked the cotton, and for this we lived in a communal barn, though families were given small shacks. These shacks were nothing more than poorly constructed wooden boxes. But they offered privacy and a fireplace for warmth and cooking. This was far better than living in the barn with those who had no family. The barn was cold, dark, and dank.

The families living in the shacks were allowed to grow their own vegetables on a small piece of land behind their homes. As well, the men of these families were allowed to set up traps in the woods, to catch small animals for food. We folk in the barn were fed daily from large pots of porridge, soups, stew containing little or no meat, and beans with corn bread.

It's not that the owners held any reverence for families. Families consisted of a mother and a father who had more and more children over the years. More children meant more workers. They were breeding us like cattle. But still, clearly, it was better than the life of a single person living in the barn. Folks were always looking to pair up, to better their lives, but not me.

The Walker Plantation was a four-hundred acre spread of Virginia's finest tobacco. Tobacco is a hearty plant and easy to grow. That does not mean you throw out the seeds and sit back and wait. There's plenty of hard work to be done, and always in hot fields without shade. Tobacco loves the sun. The soil needs to be kept dry, and there are bugs and varmints to be killed. At harvest, picking the crop is just the start of what needs to be done. The leaves need to be hung to dry, then stacked and stored to age, and protected like sleeping babies.

The main house where the Walker family lived was a two-story mansion in true Southern plantation style. It faced the main road that ran by the front gate leading onto the property.

The Walker family was Mr. Edmund Walker, Senior; his wife, Polly; and their two children, Miranda and Edmund Junior. Junior was the elder of the two by one year. Edmund Walker, Sr., was a short, squatty butterball of a man with slicked-down black hair that was thinning in the front and top. Under his button nose, he wore a small, square mustache that held a striking resemblance to a squashed caterpillar. It was a common belief held by all who knew Mr. Walker and his wife that if he had not been a wealthy man Polly Harper would never have consented to being his wife.

Polly Walker was the most beautiful woman in the county. Her black hair had a natural wave and sheen, and she had a wasp-shaped figure that was the envy of every woman in the region. She had impeccable taste and always demanded the finest, be it clothes, food and drink, furniture, or art. Mr. Walker did his best to accommodate her constant wants and wishes which, when fulfilled, kept her in a good mood and silenced her attacks upon him with her sharp and bitter tongue. As beautiful as Polly was, many were the times Mr. Walker would have traded her in for a less attractive woman with a more forgiving, less demanding, and sweet nature. Rumor was, after Polly gave her husband two children, a girl to coddle and a boy to be his heir, she felt her obligation as a wife fulfilled. It was at that point she moved into her own separate bedroom, and Mr. and Mrs. Edmund Walker were never intimate again.

The Walker children, Miranda and Junior, were eleven and twelve when I came to the Walker Farm, two and three years my senior. They were blessed with their mother's good looks, which was the only positive attributes the children possessed. They were stupid beyond belief, incapable of solving simple problems without using physical force. They were both spoiled by their parents, and as demanding as their mother with spiteful and hurtful spirits. The house slaves did their best to stay out of their way, which was not always possible. In short, the Walker children were demonic terrors.

Speaking of house slaves, there's mixed feelings about such things. On one hand, it is better to not have to work under the sun in the dirt from sunrise till sunset. But to be under the constant eye of the Walker family was a nerve-shattering experience. With the demands of Mrs. Walker and her children, life could be a living hell. Surely, many of the house slaves would think it better to toil under the sun than walk on eggshells day in and day out.

Another hazard of working at the main house, for female slaves that is, is Mr. Walker's constant sexual harassment and serious flirtation. What could a woman do? To deny him meant disaster, or possible death. Yet once Mrs. Walker found out, and she always did, the poor woman wished she were dead. It was a no-win scenario. Of course, Mr. Walker could work out his lustful intentions on the female population on the farm as well as the main house. This would take longer for Mrs. Walker to learn about, but she did. Lord help the female slave caught in such a situation with Mr. Walker. Mrs. Walker would have their hide.

The overseers were not to be trusted, either. They were known to have their way with slave women. Strangely enough, Mr. Walker and the overseers rarely touched a married woman. The husband, upon hearing of his wife being violated, would often throw all caution to the wind and take revenge, despite the consequences. Having your way with a slave woman was not worth being stabbed from behind. And such things did happen. This was another reason to pair up with a man.

The results of such goings-on led to many a child born with both white and black blood in their veins. Sadly, one drop of black blood was a cause for damnation as a slave.

Sadly, Mr. Walker, the overseers, and men like them, would refuse to acknowledge a black woman in the light of day. They would dare not so much as shake her hand in public. Yet in the dark of night where no one sees, the prejudice they held so dearly was gone. Sin loves the dark.

It was Mr. Walker's shortcomings that changed my life. Not for the better or the worst, but a change. I'd just turned fourteen, not quite a woman but on my way, when Mr. Walker took a shine to me. The good part was that knowing the boss had his eye on me, the overseers kept away from me. But he was determined to have his way with me. I avoided him the best I could, but it wasn't always possible. This went on for months until Mrs. Walker found out. How she did, I had no idea, but she did. You would think all hell would break loose for Mr. Walker or for me, or for both of us. But Mrs. Walker knew the game and played it smart. She knew how the overseers feared a jealous married man and suspected her husband possessed enough common sense to think likewise. So instead of punishing me, she arranged a marriage for me, which may have been a punishment in its own way.

Richard Brown was a tall, lanky young man, more boy than man. He was so slender there was little difference looking at him straight on as looking at him side view. He was always smiling with a look that made you wonder if he were thinking, which later I found out he seldom did, and when he did, it was never deep. Don't misunderstand; he was a sweet and gentle young man. But living with Richard was near close to living alone.

Mrs. Walker was pleased. Richard was just the type man to do something foolish if someone touched his wife. Mr. Walker never bothered me again.

At that point, life did get better. We moved into one of the shacks. It wasn't much, but it was far better than the community barn. When we weren't working the fields, I raised vegetables in the back and on all sides of the shack. Richard set up small traps nearby, which supplied us with meat. There was also fish in the local streams.

This generosity did not come from Mr. Walker's heart, but from his pocketbook. A couple was expected to drop babies, preferably one every year. Though there is no way to predict or make it so, male children were looked upon more favorably. If we were to continue living in this manner, we needed to start having children. Mr. Walker was our god and we sacrificed our children to him in exchange for our lives and our children's lives.

I had my first child that winter, a Christmas baby. We named him Willy, for no particular reason other than we liked the sound of it. He was wiry like his father, a pleasant baby and, thankfully, little trouble. The next child came the next fall, another boy. We called him Henry. He was a beautiful baby. Unlike his brother, he was plump with meat on his bones. I know you're not supposed to have favorites, but Henry was just that good looking from day one.

How odd it was to have two children by a man and not really know him. We never fought or even disagreed, and treated each other with respect. We lived day to day together, yet separate. And for all the intimacy, we remained strangers.

It was two years before any other children, more Christmas babies. That's right, I said, "babies." This time it was twins, and thankfully and finally, girls. We named them Emma May and Etta Jean. They were beautiful, and my heart's joy.

Richard always found it difficult to tell them apart, but I could. Mothers have a way about such things. Emma May had the little point on top of her upper lip; Etta Jean's lips were rounder. Little things like that a mother notices.

Life was hard, but we learned to make the best of it. Our love for the children formed a bound between Richard and me. I must admit, in time, a warm friendship existed, linking us.

I was eighteen years old, though I looked much older. Richard, only in his twenties, looked middle-aged. Our boys were growing fast; they were already working the fields. Their small hands were rough from toiling, their short childhoods taken away. The twins were still toddlers, too small to work and tied to my apron strings. It was at this time our luck was about to change—for the worse.

Emma May caught the fever. To be on the safe side, Richard and the other children moved into the communal barn. I remained in the shack, nursing our sick baby. I did what I could to nurse her back to health: vinegar baths, onions and potatoes tied to the bottoms of her feet, and much prayer. Yet the fever raged in the child, her small body as warm as a winter's stove. I sat at her bedside for days, rarely sleeping and never eating.

One night, when I was at my weakest, the door of the shack opened and in came Junior, Mr. Walker's boy. But he was no longer a boy. He was a young man, a young man with a young man's appetite. The apple didn't fall far from that tree; like father, like son.

He was drunk; I could smell it on him when he came close.

Decency dictates that I not describe the incident in detail, but you know. Just understand that whatever your imagination can conjure up, it was far worse.

Despite being married, in a weakened condition, and worst of all, nursing a sick child, he was not deterred. When he'd finished, he left me lying on the floor at the foot of my child's bed.

I woke in the morning and struggled to my feet. I sat down on the edge of the bed.

Poor little Emma May was no longer burning with fever, but was cold as ice. Tiny Emma May with the point in the middle of her upper lip was no more. The dear, helpless child, her small body unable to withstand much more, had passed on during the night. And I, her mother, was not there at her side.

The pain I felt was unbearable. I would have died then and there if not for the others in my life. For their sake, I needed to go on. I vowed not to say a word of what happened to anyone, especially Richard. I knew what he would do if prompted by jealousy.

With broken hearts, we buried Emma May and continued with our lives.

It was no more than a week later that somehow Richard learned what happened. I was working in the fields. Junior pointed me out to some of the overseers, bragging of his conquest. I don't know if Junior was arrogant, devil-may-care, or just plain foolish, but Richard overheard Junior's remarks.

Weeks went by without incident. I didn't suspect Richard had an actual plan. I imagined he just wanted to get as close to Junior as possible and kill him.

It was in one of the fields they'd already harvested. Some of the men received long knives to cut down the remaining stubs. Richard was one of them. Junior was on horseback; the overseers were on foot. The instant that Junior and his horse were far from the overseers,

Richard walked nearer to him. When he was in striking range, Richard shouted like a banshee and ran with his knife-wielding hand high in the air toward Junior. He should never have screamed. This caught the attention of the overseers. In an instant, one of them raised their rifle and shot Richard. The bullet caught him square in the shoulder. This spun him around. And loosening his grip on the knife, it went flying in the opposite direction.

Junior dismounted and stood over Richard who was moaning in pain on the ground. Junior placed his boot atop of Richard's wounded shoulder and pressed down hard. Richard's moan became screams. Then Junior picked up the long knife and thrust the blade deep into Richard's gut.

I ran toward Richard, but before I could reach him, one of the overseers took the stock of his rifle and butted me in the back of the head. This dazed me and brought me to my knees. I remained kneeling, watching them carry Richard away. He was still alive. His tortured face looked into mine for a moment and our eyes met as he passed by.

They had left the knife in Richard's gut. If they had pulled it out, he would have bled to death immediately. By keeping it in place, Richard's life and suffering would be prolonged. This fit in with their next plan.

They gathered all the slaves – men, women, and children – and made us stand around the large tree not far from the main house. I was beside myself; I figured Richard was dead by then. But I was wrong. They drove a one-horse flatbed wagon up to the tree. Richard lay in the back. He was still alive.

Two overseers jumped up onto the flatbed and lifted Richard to his feet. He couldn't stand on his own so they held him up. They tied Richard's hands behind his back.

Two other overseers tied a thick rope over one of the lower branches of the tree. A hangman's noose dangled from one end of the rope.

As they put the noose around Richard's neck, our eyes met again for the last time. I felt so sad and helpless. The look on his face was one of remorse. It was as if he were asking for forgiveness. If only he'd controlled his jealous anger, he would not have to die, his children would still have a father, and I a husband. We both knew this, but it was too late.

Without so much as an announcement, the overseer sitting on the buckboard slapped the horse. The wagon moved ahead just the few feet that was needed. The overseers let go of Richard as he slipped off the flatbed.

The blade was still in his gut; the blood poured from him. He dangled for a moment, and then he began to choke. With that, he began to kick as if he were trying to step up and ease the tension of the noose around his neck. Suddenly, his kicking stopped; the sound of choking stopped, and finally his breathing. He hung like a fish at the end of a line.

If you've never seen a hanging, you can only imagine how horrible it truly is. Now take that and multiply it by a hundred. You die slow and miserably. When it's over, your tongue sticks out of your mouth and your eyes pop out. Hanging doesn't only take your life; it robs you of your dignity.

I don't know what happened next. I fell unconscious to the ground. I do know that they left his body hanging for two days, letting the birds feast on him. Finally, they set the body on fire. The flames broke the rope and the body fell to the ground; then they buried him in an unmarked grave.

I was alone in the world with my three children. I had no idea what they would do with me; perhaps arrange another marriage with one of the single men. As much as I dreaded that, it would have been far better than what they had planned. It would seem the anger the Walker family held towards Richard extended to his family. The sins of the father condemned the children and me.

They told me to gather our things from the shack – just what we could carry, which wasn't much. They marched us off the property and stood us on the side of the road, and there we waited under the guard of two overseers. Hours passed in silence. Then suddenly a long line of chained black slaves came over the hill. When they got to where we stood, they stopped. There were a few white men on horseback patrolling the line, and two wagons at the front, one with supplies, the other holding children.

One of the horsemen dismounted and approached us. He examined our little family as if he were buying livestock. When he seemed pleased, he handed some money to one of the farm overseers. Then he mounted his horse.

I was brought to the middle of the line of slaves and linked in by my wrists. My children they put in the wagon with the other children. We began to march on.

Knowing the Walker family and their evil ways, I felt blessed. We could have been killed. Instead, we were being sold. I could only pray that our next owners held some compassion for human life. But still, how much compassion can you expect from a person who owns another person?

Chapter IV

Prayer and Caring

Etta Jean woke early and sent Liberty off to school. It was too soon to head to work; she'd left home at that hour purposely. She wanted to speak with Jaggers. What she read in the notebook the night before shined a light on what came before, but it left her with many questions.

She marched down to the Parker House Hotel and right up to the front desk. There was a different gentleman on duty, and this one seemed just as annoyed by her presence as the other. He was a horse-faced man with a long snout for looking down on people, and it was obvious he was looking down on Etta Jean. But she'd learned over the years to contain her anger at such foolishness.

"May I help you?" he asked in a condescending tone.

"Tell Mr. Jaggers that Mrs. Newman is here to see him."

"Ah, Mrs. Newman, yes, Mr. Jaggers left early this morning, but he left you this."

The clerk handed her an envelope. It was addressed to her. She was just about to open it and read it when the clerk stopped her.

"Please don't read that here. Would you kindly leave, please?"

"I just want to read it."

"Then do it outside. A colored girl at the front desk doesn't look good. Either you leave, or I call the police."

The words she'd read just the night before from her mother echoed in her mind. But Etta Jean understood the futility of arguing the point and going round and round with a closed-minded bigot. She turned and left. A block away, she stopped, opened the envelope, and read the letter.

My dear Mrs. Newman,

Forgive my running out on you like this. I've been called back to Colorado on urgent business. I can't say when I will return, just know that I will. If you need anything, don't hesitate to wire me.

I do hope you have started reading your mother's notebook. She put in so much effort into it even though she was so ill at the time. She understood it would be the only way she could ever reach out to you.

The paying off of your mortgage was just one of many gifts your mother has planned for you as well as your daughter, her granddaughter. For some reason, your mother planned never to shower you with gifts all at once, but many surprises are in store.

Again, do not hesitate to wire me for anything or for any reason.

Yours sincerely,

Jaggers

Etta Jean folded the letter and returned it to the envelope. None of it made any sense to her. But she knew this wasn't the end of it, and she wanted to see it to the end. Turning around, she started walking toward work.

At the boarding house, Etta Jean quietly went about her daily chores.

"Are you all right, dear?" Mrs. Wilkins asked. "You look so glum."

"Just lost in thought, I guess."

"Anything you'd like to talk about?"

"Maybe someday, but I just don't want to talk about it right now."

"Well, remember Auntie Faye is here whenever you need her."

That was true, Etta Jean thought. Faye Wilkins was more than her employer, she was a friend, and even more, she was a mother figure to her and her little girl – the mother she never had. She and her daughter loved Mrs. Wilkins. Etta Jean always believed she would to anything for Faye. Little did she know that soon that belief would be put to the test.

It was on a Sunday just after church. Mrs. Wilkins always served hearty and delicious meals at the boarding house, but nothing extravagant, mostly common fare. But on Sundays, she liked to serve her guests something special. This one particular Sunday, she prepared her roast with all the trimmings: salad, mashed potatoes, peas and carrots, hot buttered rolls, and peach cobbler for desert. Etta Jean was not scheduled to work, but she and Liberty were invited.

There were no empty seats around the large dinner table. There was good conversation and laughter, as if it were a holiday instead of just another Sunday in June. The aroma coming from the kitchen was heavenly.

When the kitchen help finished placing the vegetables and rolls on the table, Mrs. Wilkins entered carrying the roast. She paraded around the table one time like a royal procession filling the room with the scent of the sizzling roast.

"Mr. Wilson, would you do the honors of cutting this fine piece of meat?" Mrs. Wilkins asked as she stood at the head of the table, placing the roast down.

"With pleasure, madam," said Mr. Wilson as he stood, smiling, and then taking up the large knife and fork.

Mrs. Wilkins sat down. A cold distant stare came over her face.

"Faye, are you all right?" Etta Jean asked, sitting at her side.

"Just a little flushed, dear. It will pass."

But it didn't pass. The distant look grew farther away. There was gurgle coming from her throat and she gasped for air. She stiffened for an instant, and then the next moment she went limp and fell face down onto the table.

Etta Jean jumped to her feet. "Faye…Faye!" she cried.

The room went silent. Everyone stood up and rushed to Mrs. Wilkins.

"Give her some room," shouted Mr. Wilson. He gently lifted her up to a sitting position. He pressed his hand to her throat in true medical fashion, though he was a traveling linen salesman. "She's still breathing," he added.

"Let's get her up to her room," Etta Jean said.

Four of the men gently carried her upstairs and placed her on her bed.

"Thank you, gentlemen. Now, if you'd leave us," Etta Jean announced as she loosened the buttons on Mrs. Wilkins' blouse. She turned to Liberty. "Go down to the kitchen and tell Miriam to come quick." Liberty ran out of the room.

Miriam was a shy, sparrow of a young girl, but being the youngest of the house help, she was sure to be the swiftest.

"I want you to go and fetch Doctor Franklin," Etta Jean ordered the young woman.

"Pardon me for sayin' so," Miriam replied, "but ain't no white doctor gonna come here, no way."

Etta Jean reached into her pocket and handed Miriam twenty dollars. "Here, now he'll come. Tell him it's an emergency."

* * * * * * * *

Etta Jean and Doctor Franklin stood in the hall outside Faye's bedroom, whispering.

"She's having heart problems," Doctor Franklin said. "How bad, I couldn't say without running further tests. She won't be able to walk or talk for some time. In fact, she'll need therapy to regain her faculties." He handed her a slip of paper. "Here are three prescriptions she'll need to take daily."

"Are they expensive?" Etta Jean asked.

"I'm afraid they are, as will be the therapy."

"Well, thank you for coming, doctor."

"You're welcome. No need to see me out; I can find my way."

Doctor Franklin rushed down the stairs as if another moment would be too uncomfortable to bear. He first peered out the front door to make sure no one he knew would see him leaving.

Etta Jean went down to the kitchen. There, she sat down with the other workers of the boarding house. There was Miriam in her maid uniform; Mrs. Regina Tuttle, the cook; and Mr. Morgan Young, the handyman.

Regina was an old, rotund woman who'd gained her weight from constantly tasting her recipes, for no one ever saw her sit down to a proper meal. She'd been widowed years ago in her youth, but folks still call her Mrs. Tuttle.

Morgan was a tall, slim, older man, a jack of all trades who could fix anything. He wasn't a handsome man, and his grooming left much to be desired. But he was good-natured and hardworking. It was rumored that he and Regina had a thing going on between them, but no one could say they ever saw any signs of affection between the two of them.

"Mrs. Wilkins will be down for some time. She's not well, I'm afraid," Etta Jean told them. "She'll need full-time care."

"What is it?" Regina asked.

"It's her heart," Etta Jean replied.

Regina wore a look of doom. Diseases with long and strange names left her bewildered, but trouble with the heart…? She understood the heart. Etta Jean's eyes met hers, not a word was spoken but, they both understood the seriousness of the situation and felt the concern for Faye like she was family.

"The room next to Mrs. Wilkins…is that still vacant?" she asked Morgan.

"Yes, it is. Why?"

"I think it best that Liberty and I move into it and stay here until Mrs. Wilkins gets better."

She turned to Regina. "Will you keep an eye on Liberty while I get some of our things from the house?"

"Of course, I will," said Regina.

Again, Etta Jean looked to Morgan. "Could you please bring the wagon around front? I'd like get to some of our things from my home."

At her home, Etta Jean packed as much of their clothes as she could fit into two suitcases. She looked around and wondered if there was anything she was forgetting, then ran upstairs to get Liberty's favorite doll. She wanted to make her daughter's life as near to normal as possible.

Coming down the stairs, her eyes rested on her mother's notebook that lay on her desk. She opened one of the suitcases and gently placed it in.

Back at the boarding house in their tiny room, Etta Jean prepared Liberty for bed.

"Momma, why aren't we going home?" Liberty asked.

"Auntie Faye is very sick. She needs someone to look after her. We'll be living here until she gets well again."

"Can I go see Auntie Faye?" There was true concern in the child's voice.

"Not now, sweetheart; maybe you can in few days. Now, get into bed and go to sleep."

Once tucked in, Liberty said her evening prayers. "Dear God, bless my mommy, and my daddy in heaven, all my friends at school, and please make my Auntie Faye well again."

Etta Jean blew out the lamp and started for the door.

"Is Auntie Faye going to get well, Momma?" asked the small voice in the dark.

"Of course she is, darling. You just keep praying, and she'll be well real soon. You'll see," Etta Jean said as she closed the bedroom door.

She tiptoed down the hall. Slowly and as quietly as possible, she opened the door to Faye's dark room. The flame in the lamp was low, but still bright enough to see. Etta Jean walked to the bedside.

Faye's eyes were open, but this was no blank stare – she was alert and in the moment. The eyes of the two women met. Faye looked up with a fearful questioning expression. Etta Jean knew she had to say something.

"It's your heart, Faye. You're not well, and it's going to take some time."

Tears welled up in Faye's eyes; Etta Jean found a handkerchief to wipe them away. But for each tear she dabbed, two more appeared. It wasn't long before both women were crying.

"Now look what you've gone and done. You got me cryin', too." A small smile appeared on Etta Jean's face, but Faye's remained solemn. "Don't worry, Faye, I won't leave you. And you're going to get better. I swear to God, Faye, you're going to get better."

Etta Jean pulled a chair bedside and sat down.

"Close your eyes, Faye, and try to get some sleep. Don't worry; I'll be here if you need me."

Faye closed her eyes and was asleep in a few minutes. Etta Jean reached into the deep pocket of her apron and took out the notebook. She opened it and began to read from where she'd left off.

Chapter V

Lines of Difference

It was a long, hard march, chained as we were. I didn't know it at the time, but we walked from Virginia clear into Kentucky. The slave traders treated us well. We received good amounts of decent food. At night, they allowed my children to sleep next to me. They were frightened, but kept up appearances.

During the journey, we passed many Confederate troops, most of them marching north. We'd heard rumors of the Civil War, about how the North and the South fought over slavery, but many said it had nothing to do with slavery. As for me, I couldn't care less. I could not believe that someone would fight and die for another person, especially a black person. Slavery was all I knew and all that I saw before me and my children.

We came to the town of Colleyville. I'd never seen such a large city with its many busy streets, the rows of houses, shops, saloons, and so many people coming and going. They brought us down the main thoroughfare. At the end was a wooden stage, and next to it was a stall like you keep horses in. But there were no horses; there were slaves— black men, women, and children. There must have been a hundred of them. We were added to the number.

A man with a piece of chalk went about writing numbers on our backs and arms. He told us if we knew what was best for us we'd make sure not to smudge the numbers off.

It was early, but by midmorning, many people came. All white men, some with their wives. They gathered around the stall to inspect us. Every so often, a buyer would point one of us out. An auction worker would bring us to them for closer inspection. I was looked over quite a few times, my children only a few times. I could hope that whoever bought us was not a cruel person.

A stout little man stood on the stage. His skin was as white as his hair and beard; he looked like a ghost. He gathered the people together in front of the stage and spoke loudly through a megaphone. He began calling numbers. The workers brought up the slaves with that number on their backs and arms.

The bidding always started low, but increased slowly. I watched men, women, and entire families bought like so much merchandise. I looked at the bidders and wondered how much they would have been worth if they were up for sale. How much could the auctioneer get for them? And why was there a price on us and not them? Were they really that different? Besides skin color, I never saw the difference. Difference is in the mind.

By noon, half of us were sold. They took a break from the auction. They served liquor and plates of barbecue. Outside, the atmosphere was one of a party, but within the stall, the moments were slow torture.

When they resumed the auction, some of the bidders were drunk. There was much laughter and the bidding was high and wild.

Finally, they were down to only the group we'd come with. The auctioneer called the next number. The workers took hold of my oldest boy, Willy, and placed him center stage.

At first, I was confused. But then in a flash it dawned on me. The Walker family had pronounced me guilty and condemned me to a fate far worse than death. They had given instructions to auction my family separately.

I went insane. I took hold of the other two children and refused to let them go. I remember they were crying in my arms, and I was screaming in defiance. They couldn't have such goings-on, so they tied my hands behind my back, put shackles on my ankles, and gagged my mouth.

I looked up just in time to see Willy being taken away. Who'd bought him? Where was he being taken?

I watched helplessly as my other two children were auctioned off, each to a different buyer. The gag in my mouth barely muffled my screams.

Finally, I was brought up to the auction block. I remained bound and gagged, but this didn't upset the bidding. They seemed to understand why I was acting in such a manner. Here was a woman who'd just lost all her children; it was only natural.

Did they understand this because they, too, had children and would never want them taken away? And if they understood, why were they letting such a horrendous thing happen? Why would it be a crime if it happened to them and only an understandable misfortune for me?

I don't remember much of what happened after that. I know I was sold and placed in the back of a wagon, still bound and gagged.

I vowed that day to never obey my owners, to rebel any way that I could, to never be a "Colored Girl" again. And I swore to God that someday I would escape and find my children.

* * * * * * * *

George Branson owned a mere twenty slaves. His farm was much smaller than the Walker farm I'd come from. The family had money – old money. There was no need to produce a crop for profit. It was a self-sufficient farm, producing just what was needed to live on. George was what his neighbors described as a good Christian man. He was fair, honest, and did not treat his slaves harshly. But he did own slaves. He expected a good day's work from each of them, for which a wage was never paid, save for food, shelter, and clothing. He believed in the Good Book. That is, as far as any slave owner could believe in the Bible. So he never beat his slaves, and he gave them Sundays to rest. Many went to worship at the colored church (as they called it) five miles up the road.

His family consisted of his wife and two children. His wife, Christine, was a frail and gentle woman who showed true concern for the slaves on the farm. She would speak to the house staff as if they were one of the family. She would even give them the day off and a gift on their birthday, a hair clip for the women and a pocketknife for the men. She was a very plain-looking woman, modest in her dress but elegant in her manner.

His children were quiet, calm, and respectful of their parents and others. The oldest was Jeffery, a strapping young man of seventeen. He was muscular and handsome with blonde hair in a tall wave above his head. He was not afraid of work, and worked the farm alongside many of the slaves, without complaint.

His sister, Stella, was one year his junior. She was a smaller, compact version of her mother. Stella spent much of her time reading and doing needlework. Being self-sufficient, she seldom voiced her wishes – or her opinions.

Interestingly, Mr. and Mrs. Branson and their children, whenever they requested one of the slaves to perform a task, they always added the word "please" to their request and often called the slave by name.

Of the twenty slaves on the farm, five worked solely in the main house, of whom I was one. I was given a room just off the kitchen. It was more of a closet than a room, with just enough room for a single bed, and next to it a nightstand with a lamp.

I still held the anger of my predicament and my rebellious spirit. But I'd calmed down enough to know I needed to play the game and do what I was told to do. I would bide my time and make my move when the time was right.

At first my duties were not clear. One day I would be helping in the kitchen, another cleaning house, and yet another doing laundry. But it wasn't long till life fell into a routine.

I seldom socialized with the other house slaves, though they were friendly and kind to me. I'd seen and known their kind all my life. Slaves with a slave mentality, content with their lot. I never wanted to be content. This was the source of my misery, but also my hope.

One early morning while the world was still dark, there rose a hollering throughout the main house. I jumped out of bed, and still in my nightgown, I ran to the main hallway where the family and the house slaves were gathered.

What happened was this: a squadron of Confederate soldiers, Johnny Rebs, staggered onto the property. There were at least thirty of them. They were the last of a large troop of men, the survivors of a great battle that they lost.

They were in poor shape. Many were near death's door and needed to be carried. Their uniforms were torn, dirty, and blood-soaked. Each of them was thin as a fencepost and weak.

Mr. and Mrs. Branson greeted them, and we all went about helping wherever we could. Some of us went about feeding them and giving them drink. Others saw to the needs of the wounded. We ripped old bedsheets to use as bandages. Many of the soldiers reeled on the ground in pain; there was nothing we could do to comfort them.

I knelt at the side of one young soldier. His blonde hair was matted with dry blood, and it was encrusted on his face and neck. I washed him clean. There was already a bandage covering his eyes; he was unable to see a thing. I replaced the bandage, getting a glimpse of his charred face. He most likely would never see again. I opened his shirt to find he'd been badly hurt in the chest and stomach. He was bleeding badly, losing blood very fast. I started cleaning his wounds, and he cried out each time I touched him.

Then it dawned on me, a strange thought. Why was I doing this? Why was I helping my enemy? Here was a man who did everything in his power, up to the point of giving his eyes and his life, to have slavery continue in the land. So why was I trying to save his life?

For a moment, I considered killing him. It wouldn't take much, just some pressure on his wounds. In a moment, he'd be gone and no one would be the wiser.

Then suddenly, he called out in pain for his mother. His body stiffened and his breath became loud and uneven. He was dying. I don't know why but I held him close to me. There was a gurgling in his throat, the death rattle. He took in one last breath and let it out slow and long – his last breath – and with it he pleaded for his mother.

At that moment, I knew I could never do anyone any harm. That after putting aside all beliefs and differences, we are all the same. I wept for him, I wept for myself, and I wept for my children. I vowed someday to run away, to find my children. But to never do anyone any harm – so God help me.

Many young Confederate soldiers died that day, and surely none of them would ever be the same. We buried the ones who died, and the ones who survived hobbled away three days later.

The incident affected all of us deeply, but none so deeply as Jeffery Benson, their son. He swore his allegiance to the Confederacy and signed up the next day for active duty. It broke the hearts of his parents, but what were they to do? A week later, he was in uniform and reporting for duty.

I felt sorry for Mr. and Mrs. Branson. I understood what it was like to lose a child. In my mind, the lines of difference were beginning to fade.

Chapter VI

Full Days

Early Monday morning, Etta Jean checked on Faye. She was sleeping soundly. After seeing Liberty to school, all was quiet at the boarding house; Etta Jean made her way to the bank. Money would be needed for Faye's medicine and therapy. There was no way of knowing if Faye had any money. Even if she did, Etta Jean had no way of getting to it. She knew there wasn't much money in her account, barely fifty dollars, but if it could help Faye, she would use it. She walked up to the bank clerk and handed him her booklet.

"I'd like to close out my account," she said, opening her purse to accept the amount.

"I'm sorry to hear that, Miss...?" The clerk read the name on the bankbook. "Mrs. Newman." He opened a large leather book and looked up her account. He opened the drawer before him. "How would you like that, in hundreds or smaller bills?"

"Excuse me?" she asked.

"Well, there's just over a thousand dollars in your account. I just figured you'd want it in large bills."

"There must be some mistake," Etta Jean replied. "I believe I have only fifty seven dollars and change."

"That's right, ma'am, that's right. Fifty seven dollars and twenty seven cents, plus a recent deposit of one thousand dollars."

Etta Jean was stunned for a moment. "I'd like to speak with Mr. Boise, please."

"Mr. Boise, the bank president? I'm afraid he's busy right now."

"Tell him Mrs. Newman is here to see him. I'm sure he'll make some time for me."

Five minutes later, she was ushered into Mr. Boise's office.

"Ah, Mrs. Newman, one our favorite customers," Mr. Boise announced as he stood behind his desk, smiling. "Just the person I wanted to speak with. We need to talk about different investments for your windfall. It's a shame to let it sit doing nothing in a savings account. Money makes money, you know."

"That's what I wanted to speak with you about," Etta Jean replied. "Where did the one thousand dollars come from?"

"Oh, didn't you know? You should have received word through the post. You will receive a monthly allowance from the estate of a Mrs. Elizabeth Walker of Denver

Colorado, through the law office of a Mr. Jaggers of the same. From my communications with Mr. Jaggers, I've come to learn Mrs. Walker recently passed on. I hope she wasn't anyone close to you."

"She was my mother."

"Oh, I'm sorry to hear that. She must have loved you very much."

Etta Jean didn't have an answer for that.

"I came here to close out my account, but I see no reason to do that now. But I would like two hundred in small bills to take with me now."

"Of course," Mr. Boise said almost singsong fashion. "Don't forget, when you're ready to invest your windfall, I have many options. I'll be here whenever you need me."

After the bank, Etta Jean walked to her home. She opened the mailbox to find a letter from the law office of Mr. Jaggers.

> *Dear Mrs. Newman,*
>
> *I hope this letter finds you and yours well. As I mentioned, your mother made provision for you before her passing. She asked that I not overwhelm you and shower you with gifts all at once. So I've provided to wire you a monthly allowance of one thousand dollars at the first of each month.*
>
> *It was your mother's hope that such a process would slowly teach you how to contend with larger amounts later in your life.*
>
> *I trust you are still reading you mother's diary. Her personality and intentions will be revealed. She was a great lady.*
>
> *If you have any needs, you can wire me care of my office. I will be out of pocket for some time on business. But I will try my best to visit you before the season changes.*
>
> *Yours Truly,*
>
> *Jaggers*

Etta Jean's head was spinning. Phrases like "monthly allowance" and "learning to contend with larger amounts" swam through her mind. If a thousand dollars was the smaller amount, what did the future hold?

She walked to the pharmacy to purchase the medicines Dr. Franklin had prescribed. It was a good thing they lived in Boston. There were two pharmacies to choose from. Many small towns and cities had none. Those in need not only looked at the great cost of the new medicines of the day but great distances to cover to get to them, which was an additional expense and hardship.

The little bell over the door rang when she entered the pharmacy. A little red-faced man with a glowing bald head came out from a backroom and stood behind the counter. He neither smiled nor grimaced, just barely acknowledging her existence.

"Yes, may I help you?" he asked.

She walked to the counter and handed him the slips of paper Dr. Franklin gave her.

The man looked over the papers as he spoke, never looking up at her. "Is this for your mistress?"

"No, it's for a friend."

Then he looked up. "You understand these will be expensive?"

She nodded. She felt insulted. First he assumed she was a servant of some white woman, and then when he learned she was an independent, he assumed she didn't have the money. She understood the writing of her mother. To be considered just the *colored girl* and treated as such is the manner she'd learned to accept.

"I could have this ready by this afternoon," the proclaimed. "I'll need payment in advance. It'll be nine dollars and twenty five cents."

Asking for payment in advance was just another way of degrading her. How many others of his customers does he ask for payment in advance?

"I'll have one of my girls drop by this afternoon to pick it up," she said, taking out a ten dollar bill and handing it to the man. "Here, this should cover it. You may keep the change."

Two could play that game. She turned and left.

Next, she headed for the city hospital. Dr. Franklin not only gave her a name of an experienced therapist but a letter of introduction. At the front desk, she asked for the nurse by name. A few minutes later, the whitest woman Etta Jean ever saw came walking toward her. She was a woman in her fifties with white hair, pale blue eyes, and her skin the color of milk. Her name was Mrs. Prudence Ford, a recent widow.

"You asked for me?" the woman said.

Etta Jean handed her the letter of introduction from Dr. Franklin.

After reading it, Mrs. Ford handed it back to Etta Jean. "I suspect from the address that the woman Dr. Franklin refers to in this letter is colored and lives in the colored part of town?"

"Yes, ma'am," Etta Jean replied.

Mrs. Ford thought for a moment. "Well, I don't know. I'm not trying to be disrespectful, but I don't feel comfortable going to that part of town."

Etta Jean did not feel slighted. It was a legitimate concern. "I could have one of the men who works at the boarding house collect you and walk you to wherever you want when you're done." There still was a concerned look on Mrs. Ford's face. "I could pay you double your fee," Etta Jean added.

"That won't be necessary," Mrs. Ford said. "This man who'll walk me there and back, he's a colored man, is he not?"

"Yes, ma'am, he is."

Mrs. Ford thought long and hard. "Very well, I'll take a chance, if you will. I'll be available Mondays, Wednesdays, and Fridays. I get three dollars a visit. I get off from work here at the hospital at three o'clock. Have your man here at three on the dot."

Etta Jean nodded and smiled. "Yes, ma'am, he'll be here three o'clock on the nose."

Etta Jean was just about to turn and leave when Mrs. Ford pushed her flat hand toward her. It took a moment, but then Etta Jean realized Mrs. Ford wanted to shake hands to seal the deal. The two women shook hands. Etta Jean liked Mrs. Ford immediately.

* * * * * * * *

At first it was difficult to determine if the medicine helped Faye. She had her good days and her bad, and there was no way of knowing what caused them. For the first few weeks, the therapy was nothing more than a massage. Mrs. Ford would place Faye on her back and work on legs and shoulders. Then she'd turn her over and do the same from her toes up to the tips of her earlobes.

"Would it be good if I massage her on the days you didn't come?" Etta Jean asked Mrs. Ford.

"Couldn't hurt," Mrs. Ford responded. "Just remember to always rub inward, towards the heart. You want to push all that poison out of the places it's settled and get it out."

It seemed to make sense to Etta Jean. On the days Mrs. Ford didn't come, she'd take an hour out of her day to massage Faye. She'd even do so in the night on days Mrs. Ford did visit. As Mrs. Ford said, "Couldn't hurt."

Sometimes, Liberty would help her, messaging her Auntie Faye's feet. The child would talk constantly to the silent woman as if nothing was wrong. Etta Jean never stopped her.

One night as Liberty jabbered away to her aunt as she rubbed her feet, a deep sound rumbled in the woman's throat. It could have been nothing more than an air bubble, but it was the first sound they'd heard from her since she fell ill. There was new hope, and everyone prayed the more.

There are only twenty-four hours in a day, never enough time to do all that was needed to do. Etta Jean slept little every night, starting her day before dawn. She would look in on Liberty and then on Faye. Wash up, get dressed, and go downstairs to see to the kitchen. She was pulling double-duty seeing to everything as Mrs. Wilkins would as a manager, and fulfilling her duties as just another worker in the boarding house. As well, she had to get Liberty ready and to school on time. Then rush to her own house to check the post and see that everything was well and midday hurry back to the boarding house to oversee and help serve lunch to the few guests who paid extra for lunch. Afternoons she spent working as a chambermaid, as she had always. She'd spend time in Faye's office seeing to the business end of everything. There were bills to pay, food to be ordered, and repairs managed. After serving supper and helping with kitchen-clean up, she'd check on Faye. And then later see to Liberty.

Poor little Liberty was caught in a whirlwind away from home. Surrounded by adults, but with no help, guidance, or company to be found, and she took it all in strides without a single complaint.

Etta Jean entered their bedroom and sat on the edge of the bed, listening to Liberty say her prayers. When the child finished, her mother gently brushed her hair from her forehead and ran her hands slowly over her scalp. Liberty always loved to be stroked so since she was an infant. It had a soothing effect on her and always lulled her to sleep.

"You know, Liberty, Momma's very proud of you," Etta Jean whispered. "I know this hasn't been easy for you, living away from home. And I know I haven't been a very good mother lately."

"You're the best mother in the world," Liberty said softly.

Etta Jean continued, "Don't worry. Soon Auntie Faye will be well again, and then we can go home."

Etta Jean leaned down and kissed Liberty on her cheek. She was just about to rise from the bed when Liberty reached out and took her hand.

"Don't go yet, Momma. Stay till I fall asleep. And don't blow out the light. I want your face to be the last thing I see before I fall asleep."

"That's very sweet," Etta Jean said as she began once more to stroke her daughter's hair.

It didn't take long. Liberty's eyes soon became heavy. Her eyelids sank slowly like show curtains coming down at the end of a romantic play.

Etta Jean remained, admiring the beauty of her daughter. She was about to blow out the flame in the lamp, but then she hesitated and decided not to.

Sitting on the edge of the bed, she reached into the deep pockets of her apron, took out the notebook, and began to read.

Chapter VII

Mind and Heart

Life continued at its strange pace. Hours move by so slowly, and then add up to a blink of the eye. Time, when you want something, it moves ever so slow. When you have what your heart desires, you hold it in your hand for only a moment, and then it's gone in an instant like a blowing wind.

Some of my thinking changed during that time. Some people do certain things out of need, out of revenge, and out of sheer evil and hatred. Others do things out of obligation, responsibility, kindness, and mercy, but above all love.

The family was good people who did things out of love. They were a joy to know and work for. But they did much out of ignorance. Not stupidity, mind you; they were not stupid, but ignorant. They did not see the wrong they were doing, and so in my heart I would not condemn them. Much of my anger died on the Branson Farm, but never my inner anguish to run away, find my children, and venture to a place where we could live free.

Children, time takes them away so quickly, and in my case too soon. Poor little Emma May, a shooting star is granted more life than her. Now I must wait till I go to heaven before I can see her again. But not my other children. I will find them, by God I will. It is torture to spread out on your bed at night with their faces floating behind your eyelids, knowing that each day that those images are changing. They are out there somewhere, changing, growing. I cried the nights away when I couldn't remember the sound of their voices.

* * * * * * *

A year passed since our first encounter with the Confederate troops, the one that inspired young Master Jeffery to join the ranks. I say our first time because there were many other times Confederate troops came through. Each time they were in the worst of shape and needing help, which we gave freely. They were always on the run. By these episodes we understood the dreams of the Confederacy were fading.

With each troop that passed through, Mrs. Branson inquired about her son with each and every soldier. Surely the odds of any of the men knowing any information about Master Jeffery were slim to none. But a mother's heart doesn't see or think in those terms. They warm themselves by sparks and glimmers of hope.

The day we knew for sure the South was losing the war was when a troop of Union soldiers, Yankees, came to the farm. They looked tired and dirty, but not destitute. None of them were seriously wounded. They marched in rank, not haphazardly, and they laughed when they spoke.

I was afraid at first. I'd heard so many rumors how wicked the Yankees were. But they were gentlemen, asking politely to fetch some well water. Mr. and Mrs. Benson in true Christian fashion fed them and saw to the wounded. Again, the lines of friend and enemy, neighbor and stranger were fading.

When they left, we wished them well. Mrs. Branson prayed over them and we wish them a safe journey, just as we did for the Confederate troops.

The ties between mother and child cannot be explained, for they are invisible. They are stronger than steel and reach out father than the stars. But I never witnessed the true magic of the connection other the night Master Jeffery returned.

It was during supper. Mr. Branson, his wife, and daughter sat at the dinner table. Suddenly, Mrs. Branson dropped her spoon in her bowl of soup and brought her hand up and placed it over her heart.

"Christine, are you all right?" Mr. Branson asked his wife. "Is it too hot?" He was referring to the soup. When she didn't reply, he reached out to her. "Are you all right, Christine?"

Stella, their daughter, stopped eating and stared at them both.

Finally, Mrs. Branson spoke. "Jeffery," was all she said. She rose from her seat and headed for the front door.

"Momma..." Stella shouted, running behind her mother. Mr. Branson followed.

Outside was dark. It was only a quarter-moon, making it hard to see. Mrs. Branson ran to the front gate and off the property, followed by her husband and daughter. I ran with some of the other kitchen help to the front gate. We watched as the strange trio ran down the lane into the darkness, till we could see them no longer. For a long while, there was not a sound, only the night wind blowing through the pines. When suddenly, shouting pierced the silent air – not a scream of terror, but a shout for joy, so there was no reason to run after them, again there was silence.

We waited a few minutes, and then we could see figures moving along the lane toward the house. But now it was no longer a trio but a quartet. Four people were coming into the light.

Held closely by his mother and father with his sister close by, Master Jeffery was returning home. He moved slowly and painfully. His hair was dirty and matted against his head, and his eyes dark and sunken. His skin was smudged with filth as was his tattered uniform. He limped as he walked to the front gate. His family was in tears as they walked onto the property.

Inside, little was said. He didn't want to eat or even wash up. All he would repeat was how tired he was and how much he wanted to go to his room and sleep.

We helped him to his room. As soon as he saw his bed, he collapsed upon it into a deep sleep. His parents and I helped him out of his clothes. They left him to his dreams and went down the parlor.

After Stella went to her room, Mr. and Mrs. Branson sat up in the parlor. We left them to their privacy. They sat for hours in the dark, holding hands. Nothing else mattered. Their boy was back.

* * * * * * * *

The following morning, Mrs. Branson was up early. Every few minutes, she would look in on her boy. Each time, he was asleep. It wasn't till eleven o'clock in the morning that she found him awake. She had some of the male servants help him wash up. After a bath and a shave and clean clothes, he looked better, but not well. Each of the family members visited him. But he did not feel well enough to leave his room. They understood and asked that I prepare something for him to eat and serve it to him in his room.

I knocked ever so gently on his bedroom door. He answered in a whisper. I placed the food on a table near the window. He seemed appreciative, but in a hurry for me to leave. I noticed his dirty uniform and backpack in the corner of the room.

"Do you want me to have these cleaned?" I asked, gathering the clothes and backpack.

"No, leave them be!" he shouted in anger.

I dropped the bundle and scurried for the door.

"I'm sorry I shouted at you. I didn't mean it. Thank you for bringing me my food," he apologized gently as he closed the door behind me.

Standing in the hallway, I thought over what I'd just witnessed. When I dropped the backpack, I saw it, a bottle of laudanum. I thought little of it. Like so many people in those days, including the soldiers who took it, I had no idea what the face of the devil looked like. It was just another medicine bottle, like any other. And medicine is a good thing, right?

Within just a few days, Jeffery was again part of the family, working by his father's side, horseback riding with his sister and afternoon teas with his mother. No one of suspected anything to be wrong.

The local doctor was glad to keep Jeffery stocked with as much laudanum as the young man wanted. After all, Jeffery was a veteran who'd been wounded many times. It may take years before the pain goes away, and laudanum was a blessing from God, or so we believed at the time. It was an opiate fused in alcohol, a safe and inexpensive way of combating pain – a Godsend. Of course, the doctor worried about the problem of drinking so much alcohol, but Jeffery was a levelheaded young man and reared on moderation.

It took a long time for anyone to see that Master Jeffery was in trouble. At first, being home and eating regularly gave Jeffery the appearance of improving. But little signs began to appear that showed the opposite. He began having moments of confusion, irritability, and even anger. He was not the same sweet boy who left home. He was someone else.

His family remained tolerant for the longest time, thinking he was inwardly scarred by war, and that in time he'd come around. When he didn't, it was time to get help. They spoke to the doctor. They spoke to the pastor of their church. No one had the answer.

I was the one who figured it out. I was not in the midst of the forest, so I saw the trees. And what I saw was he was fine except during times when the delivery of laudanum or morphine was delayed. I brought this to the attention of Mr. Branson. At first, he thought it just a coincidence. But it got him thinking. He began to observe his son with my theory in mind.

Finally, to see if there was any truth in what I said, he purposely made sure the laudanum delivery was postponed for an additional day. He did not want his son to be in pain, but he had to know.

No one, not the Branson family or the house workers or even the farmworkers will ever forget that day. A monster was loose, and no one was safe.

Jeffery showed signs of being irritable days after his supply of laudanum ran out. With each day, his mood worsened. Normally, he never waited more than three days for the laudanum delivery. But through his father's influence, a week passed with no delivery. On the seventh day, he woke in his bed soaked with sweat. He was barely coherent. His body shook, and he moaned in agony. His parents tried to reason with him, only to be cursed in words and ways they'd never believed could come from their son.

Without warning, he jumped from his bed. He pushed past both his parents with a force that knocked them to the floor. Still in his nightshirt, he ran down the stairs, pushing aside anyone who got in his way. His father ran after him.

Outside, Jeffery ran for the barn. The farm slaves watched in confusion.

"Stop him! Stop him!" I remember Mr. Branson shouting.

It was an awkward situation. It took some time before the slaves understood what was needed to be done, and that they had permission to do so. A few of the male slaves took hold of Master Jeffery. It was difficult. He struggled like a wild animal to get free. He kicked, spit, and cursed all of them. It was clear once they held him, they were afraid to let him go.

His father tried one last time to get through to him, but it was useless.

"I don't want his mother to see him like this," his father told those holding him. "Let's put him in the toolshed."

It was a struggle, but they got him into the shed. They continued to hold him while some of the men cleared out all the tools. When it was clear, they tossed him in and slammed the door. Mr. Branson took a large key from his vest pocket and locked the door.

Then the strangest thing happened. Mr. Branson turned and handed the key to me.

"See to his needs, but do not let him out till this demon leaves him," he whispered to me.

I begged him not to give me such a responsibility. But he shook his head and placed his hand on mine. There was good reasoning behind his plan.

"If I or my wife take charge and have this key, it will break our hearts, for most likely we will foolishly let him out. I know your heart. You're a good person. Do this for me, and I will be in your debt." He walked away in tears.

Four of the strongest male slaves were ordered to help me whenever I needed them, and I would surely need them. I gathered some blankets, so Master Jeffery would have comfort and a place to sleep. He nearly escaped when we opened the shed door to lay the blankets on the ground, but the men were able to contain him. I also had the men cut a small opening in the shed door. Through this opening was where I planned to give Master Jeffery food and anything else he might need. I was determined to not open the shed door until Master Jeffery was free of the grip of his addiction.

That night I couldn't sleep. The thought of poor Master Jeffery alone and suffering in that shed tore at me. I left my room, went to the kitchen, and fetched a tin cup and filled it with water. Perhaps Master Jeffery was thirsty.

Outside, I found Mrs. Branson kneeling on the ground at the opening cut in the shed door. She was speaking with her son. I wanted to give them their privacy, so I stayed a few feet away and waited. After a minute, Mrs. Branson rose and started toward the house. It took her by surprise to see me standing there. We looked into each other's eyes for a moment. Then like a tree cut down in the forest, she collapsed into my arms. She sobbed uncontrollably. Then as she backed away from me, she kissed my cheek. We said nothing to each other. There was nothing to say. Words were meaningless.

I went to the shed and bent down low to the opening.

"Master Jeffery…" I called his name. "Are you thirsty?"

I held the tin cup out, and his hands reached out and grabbed it. I could hear him lap it up like a mad dog. He threw the empty cup out. I looked through the opening. All I could see were his eyes. Demon eyes they were.

Then a miracle happened. His eyes became calm for a moment, and he spoke in his natural voice.

"Elizabeth, is that you?" he whispered.

"It is," I replied.

"Don't let me out till I'm well. Don't let me out no matter what I say or do. I'm sure to kill someone; I just know it. I'm bad right now, but it's gonna get worse – I can feel it. Pray for me."

Then as quickly as it came, the natural look and voice of Master Jeffery disappeared. The demon returned. He cursed and spit at me.

I took the cup and returned to the house. In my bed, I feel asleep praying as he had asked.

* * * * * * * *

The next few days were hard on the Branson family. Night and day they heard Jeffery howl like a banshee, half in anger and half in pain. Finally, after a week, the shouting stopped. I checked on Master Jeffery often. He ate and drank little. He slept most of the day away, sleeping eight hours at a time or more. When he came to, he was calm and worn out. He still ate little, but he drank enough water to drown a man. I brought him as much water as he wanted and as often. I knew his body was trying to flush out the poison.

As for me, it was a rough time. I continued my chores in the main house, but I also put much of my time and energy into the healing of Master Jeffery. I slept little, often checking on him hourly. But the most amazing thing to happen was the transformation that took place within me. I questioned my compassion, which I honestly felt. Here I was, nursing and caring for the son of the man who owned me. In a sense, being the rightful heir, Jeffery Branson was as much my owner as his father. I'd sworn to never be treated in such a way, to be bought and sold like an animal. I hated my position in life and vowed to run to freedom at my first chance. I pledged I would find my children, and we'd be a family again and find somewhere in the world where we could live free. I felt I should find pleasure in Master Jeffery's pain, but I didn't. I found my heart filled with sympathy for him, and a need to show kindness to others. If this was a gift or curse from God, I wasn't sure. I only knew it came from God, because it was nothing I would have chosen.

As for the Branson family, my heart wept for them. The sorrow in the eyes of Jeffery's parents moved me. The torture of concern they were under made me feel sorry for them. Why was I feeling this way? These people had everything, and I had nothing, not even my own life. I had been sold separate from my children; perhaps, never to see them again. I should have been glad to see them suffer. But the heart will win over the head every time. I wanted to cradle them in my arms till all the hurt was gone. Again, this had to have been from God.

Finally, the day came when I looked into the opening of the shed and saw a tired, hurt, weak human being, but no longer a demon. I ordered the shed opened. The four male slaves under my command carried him out under their arms. He was thin and nearly used up, but he was alive and well. We took him to the main house where they carried him to his room. There the male slaves washed him, dressed him, and put him to bed. His family stood watching every moment. He slept the night through. In the morning, in his nightshirt, Master Jeffery made his way down to the dining room. He kissed his mother and father as well as his sister, and then he sat down to breakfast. They spoke little and he ate little, but it was a joy to see.

That evening, Master Jeffery came down to dinner dressed in his finest clothes. The family sat at the dinner table smiling.

Suddenly, when we were just about to serve dinner, Mrs. Branson entered the kitchen. She walked up to me and threw her arms around me. Then she undid the knot in my apron and removed it from me, handing it to one of the other kitchen workers. She then took me by the hand and led me into the dining room. She walked me to one of the empty chairs at the dinner table, next to Master Jeffery. She pulled the chair from the table and held it for me. She motioned for me to sit. Speechless, I sat down.

Mrs. Branson took her seat and folded her hands in prayer to say grace.

"Dear Lord," she said. "Thank you for your grace and mercy. Thank you for bringing Jeffery, our prodigal son, and his return to health. Thank you for Elizabeth who has given our child back to us, bless and keep her. Thank you for this food. May it bring nourishment to our bodies that we may do your bidding."

We ate in silence. We ate as a family. We were of one flesh and love.

Chapter VIII

Family Visit

Etta Jean was in the kitchen making biscuits when Miriam entered.

"There are two men in Mrs. Wilkins' office to see ya," said the young girl.

"Who are they?" Etta Jean asked.

"Don't rightly know; they didn't say. They's two handsome black men, well-dressed. They says they came all the way from New Orleans to see ya."

"Tell them I'll be right there, Miriam," Etta Jean said as she began to wipe the flour off her hands.

Etta Jean entered the office and found the two young men behind the desk. One of them was seated at the desk in Mrs. Wilkins' chair. They were similar in height and weight; both of them in their mid-twenties. Both had the beginnings of what would become thick beards. As for them being well-dressed, their clothes were clearly expensive, but gaudy: the kind of suits only a carnival barker would wear to get attention. The style of clothing only a young girl, like Miriam, would be impressed by. As for them being handsome, that, too, was debatable.

"Can I help you?" Etta Jean said coldly. She did not call them gentlemen, as she felt a true gentleman would not take such liberties in Mrs. Wilkins' office.

"And who are you?" asked the one young man seated behind the desk. The other stood next to him. They both stared wide-eyed and surprised at Etta Jean.

"Hold on, now," Etta Jean spouted. "You two come in here, without permission, and take over like you own the place. Now, before I call the police, I want to know who *you* are, and what you want."

"My name is Harry Wilkins, and this is my brother, William. Faye Wilkins is our aunt – Auntie Faye," said the seated young man.

"Faye never mentioned any family," said Etta Jean.

"She hasn't seen us since we were little," William says. "She and our mother were sisters. Our mother died years ago; no wonder we haven't kept in touch."

Harry looked at her questioningly. "That's who we are. We still don't know who you are."

"My name is Etta Jean Newman. I not only work for your aunt but she is my best friend."

"That's very commendable," Henry responded. "And we appreciate what you've done. We got word of Auntie Faye's condition, and we're here to help."

"Thank you, but we don't need your help," Etta Jean responded.

"Well, as her only family, I feel it our duty to oversee our aunt's business interests. Not that we don't trust you, but we are family and you're not," Harry said.

"Wait one minute," Etta Jean demanded. "You haven't seen your aunt since you were little, and now you show up at her doorstep, wanting to take charge?"

"Not take charge. We're here to make sure all goes well while she recuperates," said Harry.

"Show her the papers," William said, poking his brother with his elbow.

Harry took a few formal-looking envelopes from his jacket pocket. He took the letters out and spread them out on the desk. He pointed to each one as he explained what they were.

"This is a court order that gives us full rein over our aunt's property; that is, until she recovers and is able to take care of herself. And this is a letter to the courts from the doctor who examined her that states she is no condition to take care of her comings and goings."

"What doctor is that?" Etta Jean asked.

Harry looked at the bottom of the page and ran his fingers along the name as he read it. "A Dr. Franklin...you remember, you were the one who hired him."

"It's all very legal," William added.

Harry looked at her with sympathetic eyes. "There's no need to worry. No one's job is in jeopardy, especially yours; you've done such a great job. We're just here to observe in our aunt's interest. All of you can go on as before. Act as if we weren't even here."

"Where will you be staying?" Etta Jean asked.

"We can sleep right here in the office until there is an available room," William remarked. "All we need are a few blankets and a pillow each. We've slept in worse places."

Both brothers laughed out loud to this private joke.

"That will be all. You may go now," Harry said, coldly, clearly dismissing her.

There was a lot going on in Etta Jean's mind, but she knew what she would say would not make any difference to these two and would probably make things worse. This was not the time or the place. She'd bide her time, get the information she'd need, and then make her move.

****

That evening during dinner, the Wilkins brothers asked that their supper be served in their bedroom/office. This was not necessarily a hardship, but it did add to the house workers' workload, which was already a full day's worth. The brothers also gave some money to Morgan, the house handyman, to get them a bottle of whiskey. This worried Etta Jean.

That entire evening, the brothers never came out of their room, though loud laughter and cigar smoke oozed through the door.

Later that night after all the kitchen was clean from the dinner preparation, most of the guests retired to their rooms, and there was no sound coming from the brother's room, Etta Jean checked in on Liberty.

The child was fast asleep. Etta Jean felt ashamed. With all Etta Jean's household tasks, another day went by with her parenting responsibilities being ignored, though Liberty never complained. Etta Jean swore to do better for the sake of the child.

She tiptoed into Faye's room. There was no change; the woman lay on the bed motionless. Each day, Etta Jean or Miriam would sponge bathe her and move her gently to try to prevent bed sores.

It was never possible to know if Faye was conscious or asleep. You couldn't tell if she could hear you or not. Still, Etta Jean spoke to her as if nothing was wrong, as if Faye heard every word and never knowing if it was a one-way conversation or she was just talking to herself.

Etta Jean sat on the edge of the bed. She brought the blanket up to Faye's chin.

"Faye, we've got to talk. Your two nephews, Harry and William, your sister's boys. Well, they're not boys anymore. They've come with a court order that gives them power over everything here at the boarding house. That is, until you are better. I don't trust them. Faye…listen to me, Faye. I pray you can hear me. You need to get well. I'm helpless against them. You have to get well."

Etta Jean blew out the lamp and left.

****

True to their word, the brothers did not interfere with the day-to-day goings-on at the boarding house. They were rarely seen, and when they were, it was leaving the property and hours later returning straight to their room. Everyone noticed that they never wore any clothing other than the gaudy, expensive suits they arrived in.

As always, Etta Jean visited her own home once a week, checking the post and making sure all was secure. It was on one such occasion Etta Jean returned to find some major changes to the boarding house. While she was gone, the brothers had a small saloon bar delivered and constructed against one of the walls in the parlor. This was the common room where all the houseguests would gather in the evenings to socialize after dinner and before bedtime. As well, a dark upright piano stood against the far wall. There were crates of libations sprawled across the floor. The brothers were unpacking them and stocking the bar.

"What is all this?" Etta Jean asked in a demanding tone.

"Just making a few improvements," William replied.

Harry put down the bottles in his hands and stepped forward. "We're just seeing to our aunt's investment. A man likes a drink at the end of a hard day's work. Why have him gallivanting through the town at night when he can get that drink at home and for a cheaper price? The extra income will be a benefit for our dear, sickly auntie."

"And I suppose you two will see some benefit as well from this 'extra income'?" Etta Jean asked with more than a hint of sarcasm.

"It's only right we get a piece of the profits. It is our idea, and it is our effort. We paid for all the improvements. After all, the Bible says, 'the laborer is worthy of his reward.'"

"And what about the piano...?" Etta Jean asked.

This time it was William who answered. "You must admit the place could use a little livening up."

There was much that Etta Jean wanted to say, but she knew it would be like spitting into the wind. She suddenly thought of Jaggers. He was a lawyer; he would know what to do. She vowed to contact him by wire the next day.

* * * * * * * *

That evening after dinner, the houseguests settled into the parlor. Etta Jean admitted they enjoyed the change. Many of them bought a drink. A short, frumpy man came in and sat at the piano. He took off his coat under which was a shiny silk vest of red and gold. He kept his derby hat on, tilted to one side. Placing a tip jar on top of the piano, he began playing loud, joyous, fun tunes of the day.

It all seemed innocent at first, till Etta Jean noticed some men who were not houseguests drinking at the bar. She started walking to them, prepared to ask them to leave, when Harry cut her off.

"You don't think we could make any real money with just the houseguests?" His question sounded more like a statement. "Don't worry, we'll only be open to the public after dinner and then close at midnight." Then he smiled at her. "Don't you have something to do in the kitchen?" His tone made it sound more like a warning.

Later when Etta Jean walked through the parlor to get to the stairs, she noticed another addition to the room's furnishings. In the far corner was a round table. They were gambling with playing cards, and Harry was the house dealer. Meanwhile, William was behind the bar, serving them drinks as fast as they could order them. It was only seven-thirty, and the room was getting noisy. As the men got drunker, they got louder. And as they grew louder, the piano player pounded harder on the keys in order to be heard. As he grew louder, the drunken men got louder. There seemed to be no end to it. Etta Jean could only imagine how bad the ruckus would be by midnight.

Etta Jean went upstairs and checked on Liberty. The shouting from downstairs frightened the child. Etta Jean held her close and tight.

"Don't be afraid. No one will ever harm you; I won't let anyone do that, ever."

Etta Jean guided her into her bed and under the covers.

"Liberty, I want you to do something for me. This is very important."

Her daughter remained silent, waiting for her mother's instructions.

"From now on, when you get home from school, I want you to come up to your room and do your homework. Later, after you come down and eat your dinner, I want you to come straight up to your room again and lock the door. Don't open it for anyone except me. Do you understand?"

The child looked at her with fear and tears in her eyes. Etta Jean hugged and kissed her.

"There, there…it's only going to be for a little while longer, until Auntie Faye gets better. Now close your eyes and go to sleep." Etta Jean kissed her, blew out the light, and left the room, locking the door.

She entered Faye's room to check on her. There was no change. Then she went down to the kitchen to help clean up and prepare for the next day's meals. The staff was concerned about the changes, especially Miriam who'd never seen such behave in her young life.

"Just hold on," Etta Jean implored them. "This can't last for long. I promise you." Though she said this with strong conviction, none of the staff were buying it.

At midnight, the piano music stopped, and they called last call. Within ten minutes, everyone was gone, and all was quite. The brothers went to their room; Etta Jean went upstairs to bed. Quiet was finally restored.

* * * * * * * *

The next week was more of the same, only more so. Word got out there was a local place where a man could get a drink and play a game of cards every night till midnight.

There was one drawback that didn't seem to faze the brothers. Many of the houseguests became disenchanted with the arrangements. All of them were workingmen who lodged at Mrs. Wilkins' boarding house for many of the same reasons: it was a clean, quiet, affordable place for a single workingman to live. But now all that was changed.

If a man was the drinking and gambling type, the temptation to do so was just outside and downstairs from their room. Many of them went with little sleep, staying up all night. They showed up at their jobs groggy and useless. It wasn't long before many of them were in fear of losing their jobs. As well, their money was disappearing. What with the cost of drinks and gambling losses, some of them had not a cent by the end of the week. And it was interesting to all how well Harry played cards. No one ever accused him of cheating – not that anyone saw any signs of cheating. But it was amazing how well he played and how often the house won. All in all, for some, Mrs. Wilkins' boarding house was becoming a very expensive place to live.

As for the non-drinking, non-gambling men, the noise every night made it impossible to sleep. They went to work with bags under their eyes and aching backs. And as for the cleanliness they'd always appreciated, the staff was so busy cleaning the parlor from the night before, the sheets and towels were often not changed for days on end, if not weeks.

It wasn't long before men started to leave Mrs. Wilkins' boarding house in search of new lodgings.

This seemingly did not disturb the Wilkins brothers. Even after more than a quarter of the rooms were empty, they paid it no mind. Little did Etta Jean know that this played into their plans.

Etta Jean walked through the parlor as usual to get to the stairs. At first glance, there seemed to be nothing different to the room than what accrued over the past few weeks. Then Etta Jean realized what was different. There was the usual amount of men in the room, but now there were women. And these were not just any women. They had not

55

come to drink and to gamble like the men. They were dressed in a way no modest, God-fearing woman would.

It didn't take Etta Jean long to understand what was going on, as the six women who stood by the bar each disappeared with one of the men to upstairs rooms – the now-vacant rooms.

That night at midnight, Etta Jean approached the Wilkins brothers.

"I can't stop you, and you know that. But I won't have my little girl exposed to these things. I've only stayed on because of your aunt. Tomorrow, I'll be leaving with my little girl, and I'm taking your Aunt Faye with me."

She wondered if they would put up any protest. There was none. In fact, the opposite was true.

"Very well," said Harry. "We'll help you move the old lady. With you and her gone, that means two more empty rooms. I'm sure we can find a use for them."

Etta Jean went upstairs. She unlocked her door. Finding Liberty fast asleep, she bent down and kissed her daughter on her forehead.

She lowered the flame on the lamp to a low flicker and changed into her nightgown. Once in bed next to her daughter, she found it impossible to sleep. Her mind raced over what happened and wondered what she should do and what would happen to them.

She got out of bed and sat in a chair at Liberty's bedside. With the lamp flame as high as she dare put it without waking Liberty, she took up her mother's notebook and read through the night.

Chapter IX

Brent Creek

To be honest, I began receiving special treatment. The Branson family sincerely was grateful for my efforts to help Master Jeffery, and they showed their appreciation in every way they thought possible. My workload was made lighter, and I was given fewer work hours – more time for myself. Now and then they would shower me with small gifts. I'd go into my room at the end of the day and find a new dress on my bed, or shiny hairclip made of carved bone – trinkets they thought would please me.

In time, I understood that these were good people, only misinformed. They lived what they had been taught, what they learned about the black man from generations of ancestors. It was second nature to them; it was in there blood.

To everyone on the farm I became a mystery. I was living the life that all the other slaves envied and could only hope for. Yet I walked about lackadaisically with a constant dark cloud over me and a look of sorrow. My mind and heart were somewhere else; they were with my long-lost children.

It was Master Jeffery whose concern for me unburied my secret. It was in the evening, after all the chores were completed, I was walking in one of the fields. The sun was setting and the evening cool was upon us. Master Jeffery ran out to me and began walking with me.

"What is the matter, Elizabeth? You seem so sad," he asked.

"You wouldn't understand," I replied.

"Try me," he said. "I want to understand. You've done so much for me; it bothers me to see you in such a state. Haven't we been treating you well?"

I stopped walking and looked at him. I could tell he was sincere.

"Yes, you have been treating me well, better than all the other slaves. But I'm still a slave. My life is not my own. When I was sold to your father, my children were sold to other slave owners. I don't know where they are. Imagine one day someone came and took your family away from you, your mother and father, and your sister. And you had no idea where they were taken to, how they were being treated, and if they were well. What would you do?"

He went speechless. I could only hope that opening up as I did would not jeopardize my standing on the farm. And better yet that he understood my plea and took it to heart. It was a few days later when I got my answer.

Mr. Branson called me to his office. He and his wife and Master Jeffery were there.

"My son tells me you're not happy with us," Mr. Branson commented.

"It is not your fault," I said. "You've been very kind to me. But I would be unhappy in heaven if I were away from my children," I told him.

"You've done so much for us, Elizabeth," Mrs. Branson added. "We want to make it right."

"Can you read?" Mr. Branson asked, pointing to some documents on his desk.

"A little," I said.

He handed the papers to me. "This is a declaration of your freedom. Don't lose it. It makes you a free woman, no longer a slave. I got the other paper from the slave auction; it's a list of all possible slave owners who may have purchased your children." He handed me a small pouch. "This is fifty dollars in silver coins. You are now the master of your own life. We wished you'd continued working for us here for a salary. But if you feel you must leave, you are free to do so."

The papers shook in my hands as I burst into tears. "Why....?" I asked them.

"Because we want you to be happy, my dear," Mrs. Branson told me.

"No," I said. "Why do you keep slaves? I look at you, and I see good people. You've given me my freedom because you want to see me happy. That means you know that it makes a person unhappy to be a slave. I'm no different than any of the other slaves you own. Does helping your son make me special? Does it make me different from the others? No, it doesn't. They yearn for freedom as much any one of God's creations. I will not thank you for my freedom. You were the ones who took it away. And no one has that right, save for God. I pray someday you understand and mend your ways."

They were dumb-struck and said not a word as I turned and left the room. I went to my room and gathered up what few possessions I owned. Within the hour, I was walking out of the main house and down the road from the Branson farm. For whatever reason, there were no goodbyes. Had my farewell speech confused them, angered them, or enlightened them? I never knew.

* * * * * * *

It was difficult, a black woman traveling alone. I slept where I could and ate when food was available. I tried to keep off the main roads and keep to the shadows. For six months, I traveled the surrounding states looking for my children. The list from the slave auction proved to be useless. Every time I came to a new farm or plantation, I was met with failure, disappointment, and heartache.

The fifty dollars the Bransons gave me was nearly gone. I needed to give up my quest, at least for the time being, and find a way to make a living.

I came to a small town in Virginia name Brent Creek. There wasn't much to the town – a bank, a saloon, a hotel with a restaurant, a supply store, and a sheriff's office with a four-cell jail. Two years earlier, coal was found in the surrounding hills. This was the only reason there was a Brent Creek.

When the war broke out, all the young white men who worked the coal mines signed up to serve in the Confederacy. The mine owners needed workers desperately. They thought of using slave labor, but the tunnels of the mines were low ceilinged and not very wide. There was no way an overseer could keep an eye on the slaves. And no man who is made to work for nothing will work unless forced to. Punishment only left you with workers who couldn't work. There had to be an alternative. There was, and it came in the form of immigrants who needed work and would work for low pay. Most of them came from Russia. Some came with their families, but most were single men who needed caring for by a woman. And that's where I came in.

Most of the mine workers did not live in town. They lived on the outskirts of town in canvas tents – an entire city of tents outside the city limits. They would only go into town for their supplies, and on Saturday nights to the saloon to drink. They were paid by the amount of coal they harvested which gave them the incentive to work harder.

With what little money I had left, I bought a canvas tent to live in and set it up on the edge of the tent village of miners on the outskirts of the town. I purchased a large caldron and a fair supply of lye soap. I spread the word around that I was taking in laundry. These were men who had no woman to look after them. Laundry was a mystery to them. Within a week, I had more work than I could handle, I was turning away work. I had to take on extra hands to help me. This came in the form of two black girls, sisters, Minnie and Teresa, both in their twenties. They worked in the restaurant as dishwashers, but I had no trouble luring them to work for me. I offered them twice what they made at the restaurant. They stayed with me in my tent till I put aside enough to buy them a tent of their own, which we pitched right next to mine.

Though there were two years' difference between the sisters, Minnie being the oldest, the two looked the same age. They were a shy duo, skinny and dilapidated as any plantation slaves, dressed in rags and poorly groomed.

Though we were not getting rich, we were making a good living. But this was only the beginning. I had other ideas.

I thought about what other services I could offer. I bought scissors and a razor. I began offering haircuts and shaves. Again, this went over well, especially on a Saturday afternoon when many of the men planned to go into town. Many of them would visit the working "ladies of the night" on Saturday evenings. Though it was far from mandatory to look their best for these women, it became the practice to go into town wearing clean clothes and sporting a haircut and a fresh shave.

I paid Minnie and Teresa well, but I also showered them with gifts for jobs well-done, not only as an incentive, but to get them to be more presentable. When I first found them, they were two frumpy women who cared little for themselves. I bought them new clothes, got them to take pride in themselves. Once they did, they never looked back.

Again, business increased, so it was time to take on another worker. This was to be Christina, a white girl of twenty who'd been jilted by her fiancé. She was a slender blonde beauty whose good looks were covered in soot when I found her. And the stress of a hard life was already starting to take its toll.

It was an old story. An older, handsome man takes advantage of a young woman. He promised her love and marriage, in exchange for the wifely duties without the ring. She traveled with him from work camp to work camp, cleaning and cooking for him, and all the rest. When he tired of her, he left her stranded in Brent Creek.

There were few alternatives for a young white girl on her own so far from home in a strange town full of mostly men. She could find another man to take care of her or she could work the saloon. These prospects frightened her, but it was that or starvation. To Christina, my offer of work with dignity was a Godsend. I set her up in the tent with Minnie and Teresa, and in no time the three became good friends and excellent workers.

Though there were fewer families living in the work camp than single men, I made a good profit as a midwife – a knowledge I'd picked up in my years on the farm. Women were constantly having babies and my services were all that was available.

In time, I took on more workers to handle the workload. Minnie, Teresa, and Christina were not only my main workers, but they'd become what could only be called my managers overseeing the other workers, for which I paid them well.

It was then that I came up with my most lucrative scheme. I noticed that many of the men on their Saturday night visits into town would treat themselves to a hot meal at the town's only restaurant. Still, this was a luxury few men could afford or wanted to spend their hard-earned money on. Because of their demanding work schedule, many of the men had no time to cook their food, even if they knew how. So many bought supplies in town, food they could eat on the go without cooking. I bought another tent, a large one, and began cooking simple meals the men could purchase. It wasn't much, mostly beans, stews, soups, eggs, and biscuits, but it was far better than what they were eating, and at a reasonable price.

It was getting so that except for their Saturday night excursions to town, there was little to no reason to go into town, except to buy a plug of tobacco or a bottle of whiskey. I was doing well throughout the camp; I was everybody's friend. Little did I know that at the same time I was making enemies. My luck was about to change.

It was a Sunday morning when the camp was quiet. Not that folks were at church, because there was none, nor was it respect for the Sabbath. The mine owners knew the men had spent the night drinking the night before, so rather than be overloaded with Sunday morning accidents, they allowed the men to come in later at ten o'clock.

I was visited by the sheriff and the mayor of Brent Creek. To be honest, I didn't even know the town had a mayor.

They were blunt and straightforward. Without any dillydallying, they placed their cards down. It seemed the shopkeepers complained about me. I was taking much of their business away, the restaurant especially. They didn't mind my midwife business; they had no experience in that. But they were losing money on my cooking food for the men. As for my barbering, a professional barber was thinking about opening a shop but told the mayor he wouldn't if there was any competition. As for the laundry business, the shop owners were kicking themselves for not thinking of it first. Now they wanted that business, and it would only work if I were out of the way.

This would leave me with just the midwife business, which was far and in-between, and would not generate enough income for myself, let alone all the lives that now depended on my business.

Being a Christian woman, I will not repeat my answer to these men. And I pray the Lord will forgive me, and like Isaiah, send an angel to press a red-hot coal to my lips to wash the iniquity from my mouth. Let us just say I told them, "No!".

Surprisingly, they didn't argue. In fact, they didn't even say a word. They just turned and rode away.

"You've been warned," said the mayor over his shoulder.

I did not take his words lightly; I took it as a threat. I warned all my workers to keep an eye out for anything strange. But I was only kidding myself. I've learned in this life that what is to be will happen no matter what. You cannot keep an eye out forever. Eventually, you have to close your eyes to sleep, and that is when they will come.

It was on a weeknight, after midnight when all the camp is asleep and all is quiet. I woke to the sound of roaring in my ears. I'm sure I have a guardian angel because there is no other reason I did not die in my sleep. The noise woke me. I opened my eyes to a bright light, but it was not the white light of the morning sun. It was the glaring yellow and orange of hot flames. My tent was on fire. I jumped from my cot and instinctively ran out. The smoke was in my lungs, and I fell to the ground, choking.

I looked to the other tents for some help. The tent next to mine was in flames.

"Minnie…Theresa…Christina…!" I shouted over and over till they woke and ran from their tent. Christina emerged with the hem of her nightgown on fire. She ran about frantically. I took hold of her, pulled her to the ground and rolled her in the dirt till the flames were out, but her legs were badly burned. She would be scarred for life.

In time, others woke and came to help. They did what they could, but there was not enough water in the camp to put out the fire.

In the morning, the girls and I sat on the ground staring at the ruins. Our tents and all our belongings were nothing but a pile of ashes. And the two other tents were gone, the one we used for laundry and the other where we cooked the meals. All our supplies were destroyed, as well as all our equipment.

In just a few hours, our lives were gone. I refused to cry, but I swear I wanted to. I felt so lost and hopeless. How would I ever find my children now?

I was angry. I wanted to take revenge, but how? I want to call out to God, "why?" But before I could, the Lord sent an angel to give us new hope.

Chapter X

Cleansed by Fire

It was difficult moving Faye to Etta Jean's home. Being completely immobile, she had to be carried. Morgan and a few men who'd been regular guests at the boarding house helped. None of them lived there any longer ever since the changes the brothers made.

In addition to not wanting to expose her daughter to such dark ways of life, Etta Jean couldn't see herself remaining in that kind of atmosphere. So she quit her job. She should have worried, but her monthly allowance sent from Jaggers' office in Colorado was far more than enough to survive on and to pay for Faye's medication and therapy. In fact, the allowance was enough that Etta Jean would not have to work at all. But not wanting to look a gift horse in the mouth, she realized there was always the possibility the allowance would stop someday. She knew she needed to stay in the frame of mind she was in.

The only person who had no qualms was Liberty. The child was so glad to be home and back in her old room. The time spent at the boarding house, especially the last few weeks, had been trying. She was a brave little girl and never expressed her true feelings, but she was always afraid once the Wilkins brothers took over.

Mrs. Ford began visiting Etta Jean's home to continue Faye's therapy. Though many might disagree, those who knew Faye well felt she was getting better. There seemed to be a look of awareness in her eyes that had been long missing from them.

Sad to say, money or not, few lawyers would take Etta Jean, a black woman, seriously. It was Mrs. Ford who went about enquiring at the offices of different lawyers as to what could be done to be rid of the Wilkins brothers. Every lawyer told her the same story: there was little that could be done, and if Faye did not show signs of getting well soon, the property could be put in complete control of the Wilkins brothers. It would be legal robbery.

Desperate, Etta Jean sent a letter to Jaggers, explaining the situation in great detail. She received a quick response.

> *Dearest Mrs. Newman,*
> *I hope this letter finds you well. I have read your letter of concern and have studied it carefully.*

I'm afraid I agree with the other lawyers you have consulted with in your area. If your friend's health does not improve after a certain amount of time, depending on the judge hearing the case, her nephews can take over complete control of her business. And worst of all, if these two men have any money to grease some palms, it is sure to happen.

But might I make one suggestion? Do not fight them. Allow them to do this dastardly deed. Allow them to take complete control. Once they do, offer to buy them out. If they are the type of men you've described, they may eagerly accept a cash payment, which will make them wealthy men without having to work for it.

Have the property appraised and get back to me about the cost, and then you can make them an offer. If they accept, I will send the money from your mother's account. I have the authority to approve any amount, providing it is in the interest of making a profit. For this reason, I warn you that you must become partners with your friend. Have a local lawyer work up the papers. If you plan to buy the property and then give it to your friend as a gift, I won't be able to approve the funding.

Again, I hope you are well. Please, keep me informed as to the direction of these events.

Yours in waiting,

Jaggers

Again, Mrs. Ford's help was well appreciated. An appraisal can be costly. But the price is considerably lower if ordered by a white woman.

Sadly, an appraisal looks only at certain aspects of a property – where it's located, its size, the age and condition of the structure on the property. The potential to make money doesn't come into play. The years of Faye's hard work to make her boarding house successful were never considered. The final appraisal price was twelve hundred dollars. But again, that was the value of the building. Etta Jean knew the brothers were making money. She would need to offer them not only the price of the building but the profits they were making from their in-house business. She decided that an additional thousand dollars would suffice – twenty-two hundred.

Etta Jean immediately wrote Jaggers. He approved up to twenty-two hundred dollars to offer the brothers.

Etta Jean went to the boarding house midafternoon when she was sure there would be few to no customers. When she arrived, the bar was closed and all was quiet. She went to the office and knocked on the door.

"Go away!" shouted one of the brothers. They still were using the office as their sleeping quarters, rather than give up a room that brought them profit.

Etta Jean pounded hard on the door, over and over, till Harry opened the door. His angry look left his face when he recognized her. He became all smiles.

"Well, well...come back to ask for your job?" Harry asked. "Come in, come in."

He moved out of the doorway to let her in. His brother, William, was just waking. They both looked ragged, having slept in their suits. Harry sat behind the desk putting on his shoes. William sat barefoot on the couch.

"So, was I right: you want to come back?" Harry asked.

"What makes you think we want you?" William growled.

"I'm not here for a job," Etta Jean replied. "I'm here on you aunt's behalf. I've come to make you an offer to buy you out. What would it cost to see the back of you two? Mind you, I've had the property appraised."

Harry finished tying his shoelace. He sat up, smiling. "Go ahead, we're listening. Make us an offer."

"I'm willing to give you eighteen hundred for you to pack up your bags and leave. That's far more than the appraisal came to."

Harry began to laugh. He looked over to his brother, and both of them burst into a fit of laughter.

"You know how much we make in just a night?" Harry said, once he controlled his laughing. "There's the liquor, the gambling, and the women, not to mention this." He took a small box from his desk drawer. He opened it and held it toward Etta Jean. She looked in to see a round, black blob. "That there's opium. We can make eighteen hundred in a month on just that." He looked into Etta Jean's eyes. "Oh, I know what you're thinking. Yeah, just about everything we do is against the law in this part of town. But who's gonna say anything? You got a fine life and pretty little daughter. You don't want to put her in jeopardy now, do ya?"

It wasn't direct, but it was a threat, and she knew it wasn't an idle one.

Etta Jean made another offer. "I'll up the price to twenty-two hundred."

Again, they laughed at her.

As angry as she was, she did not want to take it any further. She turned and left the room. She could hear them still laughing as she walked down the hall and out the front door.

****

It was late at night and something woke Etta Jean from her sleep. She sat up in bed. She heard it again, a loud pounding on her front door. She rushed out of her bedroom and quickly looked in on Liberty and Faye. They were both fine. The pounding continued. Perhaps the Wilkins brothers were making good on their threats. She rushed downstairs to the kitchen where she grabbed the biggest and sharpest knife she could find. She slowly walked across the parlor toward the front door. Again, the pounding resonated from the front door.

"Who is it?" Etta Jean whispered, placing her ear to the door.

For a moment, there was no sound. Then she heard crying. A woman was crying on the other side of the front door.

"Who is it?" Etta Jean repeated.

"It's me, Etta Jean. It's me...Miriam."

When she opened the door, Miriam fell into her arms in tears.

"Miriam, what's wrong?" Etta Jean asked; hold the young girl up as best she could.

Etta Jean guided her into the parlor and sat her down. She ran to the kitchen and brought her back a glass of water. Miriam was shaky, but she soon calmed down a bit.

"I couldn't take it anymore," Miriam cried. "I'm sorry to bother you, but I couldn't think of any other place to go."

"It's all right," Etta Jean reassured her.

"I try to be a good girl," Miriam pleaded. "But they took advantage of me."

"Who did?" Etta Jean asked.

"The brothers did," Miriam said reluctantly. "That's why I did what I did."

"What did you do?"

Still in tears, Miriam pointed to the window. There was a faint yellow glow coming from outside, from behind the curtains.

Etta Jean walked to the window. She pulled the curtains apart. There was a flickering glow in the sky behind the buildings in front of Etta Jean's house. There was clearly a fire off in the distance."

"I couldn't take it anymore," Miriam cried, her entire body shaking. "They took advantage of me. I'm a good girl, you know?"

Miriam rambled like this for some time, till amidst the confusing talk, Etta Jean was able to make sense of Miriam's account.

As far as Etta Jean could tell, Miriam was molested, if not raped, by one or both of the Wilkins brothers, on more than one occasion. With all the women at the bar so willing, it was the most innocent and least willing that they wanted.

Miriam did not tell Etta Jean the sordid details, not that she wanted to hear them. But it was understood.

"There, there, Miriam. No one's going to hurt you anymore."

Though Etta Jean spoke from the heart, nothing she said soothed the young woman's fears.

"I did it," Miriam finally confessed.

"You did what?" Etta Jean asked.

Miriam pointed to the window. Not understanding, Etta Jean opened the front door. Off, not so far in the distance, a fiery glow lit up the sky. Etta Jean tightened her robe around her, stepped outside, and began down the walkway. She ran to the corner with Miriam close behind. From the corner, she could see the boarding house. It was engulfed in flames. Etta Jean turned, took hold of Miriam, and guided her back into the house.

"Tell me, what happened?" she demanded of Miriam.

The young woman was sobbing and slow to respond. "They tried it again…the brothers. They dragged me from my room to their office. I wasn't gonna take it again. I grabbed the lamp and threw it at William. The lamp broke, and he went up in flames. Harry tried to save him, but he caught fire, too. Before I could get out of the room, everything was on fire. I was so scared that I started for the door and then out of the building. I screamed, 'fire, fire!' Thankfully, everyone else in the building got out. We stood in the street watching the building go up. When the fire truck came, I was afraid they'd ask questions. I'm sorry to be so much trouble, but I didn't know where else to go."

"It's all right. You can stay with us till we figure out what to do," Etta Jean said, guiding Miriam up the stairs. In Etta Jean's bedroom, Miriam collapsed onto the bed, still in her clothes. She cried herself to sleep in only a few minutes.

Etta Jean went to check on Liberty. The child was asleep with not so much as a flutter from her eyelids. Then she went to see how Faye was. At first glance, it looked like nothing had changed in her condition. But with closer inspection, Etta Jean could see Faye's face in the light of the burning boarding house that poured into the room through the window. It was only a slight difference, but a strange one, indeed. There was a small, but unquestionable smile on the woman's face. She did not respond to Etta Jean, but it was clear she somehow knew what was happening and was glad.

Etta Jean went downstairs. It would be morning in a few hours, when she'd make breakfast for Liberty. She sat in the chair by the window. The light of the fire still coming through the window illumined the room enough to read by. She took her mother's notebook, opened it on her lap, and began to read.

Chapter XI

New Direction

I couldn't feel any lower than I did at that moment. Everything I'd worked for was in ashes, and everything I hoped for now seemed far from my reach. I have always been a strong person, always ready to pick myself up and dust myself off and try again. But this was like nothing before. I was at the bottom. I couldn't see anything below me, and I didn't have the strength to look up. Then a deep voice resonated behind me.

"Excuse me, but are you Elizabeth Walker?" said the voice.

I turned to see the most distinguished white man I'd ever laid eyes on. He was dressed in the finest of traveling clothes: shiny, knee-high boots; a ruffled shirt; and a heavy, dark, wool coat. A warm smile adorned his clean-shaven face. Eyes of blue shined out gently from under the wide brim of a cut-top hat that partially covered his sandy, full hair.

"It seems I've come at a bad time," he said.

"I've seen better days," I said. "What do you want?"

"I've been looking for you. I've heard you're a woman of many talents. My name is Duncan Monroe. I'm an entrepreneur."

"You're what…?" I asked. I'd never heard the word before.

"An entrepreneur. It's someone who makes money investing in businesses."

"You must have a lot of money."

"More than my share, I'd say."

"Well, Mr. Monroe…"

"Call me Duncan."

"Well, Duncan…I still don't know what you want of me."

"I've recently purchased some land in Colorado. I plan to mine it. Not coal like here, mind you. I believe there's gold to mine. We can all be rich."

"That's all well and good," I said. "But what do you need me for?"

"You're a woman of many talents. I'm traveling with a hundred men by wagon train to Colorado. They need to be fed and cared for; you have that ability."

"When you say 'cared for,' I don't do things like that." I said.

"There'll be nothing like that," he laughed. "You'll just be doing what you've been doing here at the camp, only it will be on the trail. And when we reach Colorado, if you'd like

to stay and continue doing what you're doing, you can. In fact, I'll make a deal with you. You'll be the only one to offer services to the workers. No one opens so much as a can of beans without your say-so."

"If I take up your offer, I'll need my three girls to come with me," I demanded.

"Absolutely," he said, "whatever you need to make it happen."

"And the pay...?" I asked.

"Shall we say twenty dollars a day plus expenses? And when we reach our destination, you can set it up like you had here."

I took my time answering. The price was more than fair, but I didn't want him to think of me as a pushover. But when I looked at the damage the fire did to my business, we both knew, fair or not, it was the only offer available to me.

"Very well, we'll give it try," was my answer.

He smiled. "Good. We leave Monday morning. I'll keep in touch. If you need me, I'll be at the hotel. Oh, and by the way, don't mention this to anyone. If the powers that be knew I was taking a hundred of their men away, there might be trouble."

He reached out his hand to shake on the agreement. I have to admit, it took me by surprise. To be offered a handshake was to treat me with respect and to treat me like an equal.

* * * * * * * *

The next day, two wagons were delivered to us. One was for me and the other girls to travel in. The other was to be a kind of chuck wagon to haul the food needed for the first leg of the journey – food for more than a hundred people.

This was the downfall of our plan. The amount of supplies I ordered in town was suspicious since I'd lost my business. It was more food supplies than I'd ever ordered. As well, there were pots and pans and utensils. It was all very suspicious. Those in power understood this, that something was afoot. Besides, there was rumor in the camp. There are always those who will side with the opposition because there is a reward for doing so.

Four men showed up with rifles. They were sent by Mr. Monroe to protect us. For the next few days all they did was guard us, watching our every move with their guns in hand – always watching.

Finally, Monday came. In the early morn, our four guards showed up on horseback. As if like magic, other wagons appeared and lined up in front of our two wagons. I drove one with Christina at my side. Minnie and Teresa were in the wagon with the supplies behind us, and *there were many men on horseback. By full sunup, we were a long wagon train ready to move, with Mr. Monroe on horseback at the lead.*

Before we were able to move, a group of men with guns in hand came riding toward us and stopped before Mr. Monroe.

"Where ya think you're goin'?" asked the mayor with the sheriff at his side.

"We don't want any trouble," said Monroe, but I could see that's what the mayor and his men came for. "We just want to be on our way."

"You're takin' a good chunk of our workforce," the mayor said.

"It's a free country, and these are free men." Monroe argued.

"They ain't even from this country. Most of `em can't even speak English. The only rights they have are the ones we say they have."

"Step aside, Mayor!"

"All these men are crack shots," said the mayor, pointing to the gunman at his side. "Give it up, Monroe; we got more firepower than you."

"Yeah, but I got more brains than all of you put together. Now, let us get by or you'll be sorry."

The mayor laughed. Monroe raised his hand. "I'll give you to the count of ten, Mayor." This wiped the smile from the mayor's face. The gunman put their hands in position to draw their guns. The tension built as Monroe began counting.

"Ten..." Monroe shouted, dropping his raised hand.

At first nothing happened. No one so much as drew their guns. Then the next second, the ground shook from a mighty blast. The explosion came from the center of the town. Everyone turned to the town to see black smoke and pieces of wood fly into the air.

"That was your livery stable. Don't worry we took the horses out first," Monroe said. "Now, get out of our way or you'll lose another piece of your town."

The mayor and his men were dumbfounded; they didn't say a word. Monroe held up his hand again.

"I'll give you to the count of ten," Monroe said, holding his hand on high.

"All right, Monroe, you win. Let them pass, boys."

Monroe waved his hand vigorously before lowering his arm. The group of gunman moved out of the way. Monroe signaled to move forward. We were on our way.

* * * * * * * *

The going was slow that first day; it took hours before the town of Brent Creek was well behind us and out of our site. When the sun was halfway down in the west that was when we stopped for the night. In true wagon train fashion, we formed the wagons in a circle. Many of the men went to fetch firewood for the campfires. This is when my girls and I got down to work. Cooking for a hundred hungry men is hard work, but not as difficult as you might think, if you have the right equipment – and we did.

It took two hours to prepare the meal, one hour to serve it, and twenty minutes to eat it. When they finished, we got to eat, also. That was when Mr. Monroe came to talk with me.

"That was a fine meal you made for us. You really know your job. You've proven to me I made the right decision when I hired you."

"Well, thank you, Mr. Monroe," I said.

"Remember, call me Duncan."

"Well, thank you, Duncan."

"Well, you have a good night's sleep," he said.

"'Good night's sleep,'" I laughed. "We got dishes and pots and pans to clean, if you want breakfast in the morning. And we'll have to get up an hour earlier than anybody else, if you want breakfast."

He smiled, "You really do know your business." He started to walk away. "Goodnight, Beth," he said. I didn't say anything, but no one had ever called me Beth.

"Goodnight, Duncan," I called back.

Christina leaned over and whispered in my ear. "I think he's sweet on you."

"You're crazy," I told her.

"That may be true," she said. "But he's sweet on you."

Chapter XII

Game for a Change

The authorities came by a few times to ask questions but concurred it was an accident and not arson. The only victims were the Wilkins brothers whose bodies were burned nearly beyond recognition. Etta Jean walked down to the site of the boarding house to see what condition it was in. There was nothing salvageable, hardly one brick on another. It was now an empty lot of chard bricks.

Without a place to work, Etta Jean wondered what she'd do with her life. There was her allowance, which was large, but she had no idea if or when that might suddenly stop.

Miriam had no place to go so Etta Jean moved her into the parlor where she slept on the divan. She gave Miriam a few dollars to get some clothes, as everything she owned was lost in the fire. To show her gratitude, Miriam did all the cleaning and cooking, and tried to stay out of everyone's way.

Liberty was the most content with the situation. She was back home, in her own room, and everything was normal again. Etta Jean was so glad her child was no longer exposed to the kind of place the boarding house had turned into.

As for Faye, miracles started to happen daily. The hint of a smile that appeared on her face the night of the fire turned larger and clearer. There was liveliness in her eyes that hadn't been there for so long. But most hopeful of all were her eyelids. She could open and closed them with ease and regularity.

Mrs. Ford set up a way of communicating with Faye. "I want you to blink your eyes once for 'yes' and twice for 'no,'" Mrs. Ford said, looking down into her patient's eyes. "Can you hear me?" Mrs. Ford asked. Faye squeezed her eyes tightly for a full two seconds. "Are you in any pain?" Faye replied with a clear closing of her eyelids twice.

Etta Jean was in the room at the time and broke into tears. It was good to see the progress, but it was a bittersweet victory, for there was such a long and uncertain road ahead.

Mrs. Ford's visits became more frequent. The massages and stretching of Faye's limbs continued, but more was added to the therapy. They would all ask her questions which she answered by blinking. This was to keep her alert and her mind working. In the daytime, they propped her up in a sitting position. But the most radical change in her therapy was to try to help Faye relearn how walk and talk.

Mrs. Ford started Faye on some breathing exercises. She held a thin silk scarf in front of Faye.

"Now, just try to move the scarf with your breath," Mrs. Ford instructed Faye.

The first few tries were discouraging. As hard as Faye tried, she could not move the silk scarf with her breath. Only a deep, gravelly grunt resonated in her throat. But even that was a big improvement. In time, with great effort and determination, Faye was able to move the silk scarf. Just slightly at first, but with a few days' practice, she had it waving like a flag. And in time, she could move the scarf in any direction she wanted: up, or to the right or left.

"Now, I want you to blow on the scarf again, but this time put your lips together and make the 'p' sound – like this 'pah,'" Mrs. Ford demonstrated for Faye. Again, it took a few days' practice, but in time Faye got it. Then they moved on to the "b" sound and from there, other sounds. At times Mrs. Ford used a feather for sounds that weren't so clearly pronounced, like "h," "e," and "o." Then she got her humming to get the "m" and "n" sounds. At first, it sounded like no more than nonsensical grunting, but soon the sounds became clearer. It was obvious the therapy was working.

The next part of the therapy was the most challenging. It was difficult to teach Faye how to use her muscles again. The amount of effort just to sit up straight was monumental. Not that the positions were painful to her, but any way they posed her, she still had the posture of a ragdoll.

Etta Jean checked on her bank account; there was no allowance sent. She understood, as she had always believed, that some things are too good to be true and you must only rely on yourself. This came from being raised without any family, especially parents.

For this reason, Etta Jean decided to take drastic measures. With the Wilkins brothers out of the way, there was no doubt Faye Wilkins was the owner and in sole control of her property. But Faye was in no condition to govern herself, let alone her property. Etta Jean decided to put this to their benefit. With the help of Mrs. Ford, they appealed to the courts that Mrs. Faye Wilkins would be in dire straits if she did not sell her property, as the money would be needed for her care and benefit. It was a costly and lengthy procedure, but in the end they were given permission to sell Faye's property.

But there were restrictions. The court would assign Faye a legal representative to oversee the sale of the property, and the profit would be put in escrow and used only for the benefit of Mrs. Wilkins. They would need invoices for every visit by Mrs. Ford and everything they purchased for Faye. Though they couldn't touch this money for anything other than Faye's benefit, it would take some burden off the household.

It was then Mr. Hagar entered the picture. He was the lawyer assigned by the court to oversee the sale of the property. He was a dumpy little man with a crown of red hair circling the sides of his bald head and a round, white face that looked like biscuit dough. His suite was of the highest quality, but old and worn. He annoyed Etta Jean by his tendency to be so overly friendly it was clearly an act. This made her wonder about Mr. Hagar and dread his visits. It seemed he knew he was chaffing people but used it to his own advantage, putting folks off guard.

He visited Etta Jean twice to discuss the matter. Since the property no longer had a building on it and only the land was up for sale, the assessment was low – only one thousand dollars. And ten percent of that would be Mr. Hagar's fee which, after some investigation, Etta Jean learned was a fair cost.

For a little over a week, Etta Jean heard nothing from Mr. Hagar. Till one day she received a letter from his office stating he had found someone interested in Faye's property and willing to offer the amount the property was assessed for. The letter also stated that if she wanted to proceed with the sale to send him word as to when the signing could be. They would have the signing at her home for her convenience. Mr. Hagar would then make all the arrangements.

Etta Jean wrote Mr. Hagar she would be ready to sign the papers the following Friday at one o'clock. She also wrote that she had a few questions before she went any further with the sale. But there was no further word from Mr. Hagar.

The following Friday at the very moment the clock in the parlor struck one, there was a knock on the door. Mr. Hagar had brought one of his secretaries, a Mr. Cutter, to be a witness. Mr. Cutter was the exact opposite of Mr. Hager. He was as tall and scrawny as a scarecrow. He wore a plaid suit that was too tight, even for him. The sleeves and pant legs were too short, exposing his wrists and socks that didn't match. As much as Mr. Hagar was hard to shut up and continuously talking, Cutter was as silent as a picket fence.

They all sat around the dining room table: Mr. Hagar, Mr. Cutter, Mrs. Ford (also as a witness), and Etta Jean. Miriam came in and offered tea to anyone who'd want it.

"No, thank you, my dear young lady," Mr. Hagar said in a desperate tone, as if he were in a hurry and had not time for such social graces that would distract him from his duties.

Mr. Hagar put on his reading glasses and spread the papers on the dining table in front of Etta Jean.

"Now this here paper, Mrs. Newman, gives you the right to act on Mrs. Wilkins' behalf. As you can see, it is already signed by the judge. If you would, please sign your name here under the judge's signature."

Etta Jean read it slowly, which seemed to annoy Mr. Hagar.

"It's just your everyday transfer of power, Mrs. Newman, nothing you'd need to take notice of."

This annoyed Etta Jean, and she felt it a bit degrading. But she kept it all inside, and continued to read the document.

It was only one page and was easy to understand, save for a line or two of legal gibberish. Etta Jean questioned Mr. Hagar on these points. His answers were no clearer than the lines in question.

Believing there was no other way, Etta Jean signed the document. Mr. Hagar had Mrs. Ford and Mr. Cutter sign it as witnesses.

Then he placed the bill of sale before Etta Jean. This was eight pages long and as complicated as the schematic to a steam engine. And as hard as Etta Jean tried to read and comprehend it all, there were lines that she couldn't understand. Again, when she questioned their meanings, Mr. Hagar's explanations left her more puzzled. Mr. Hagar phrased the legal jargon in such a manner and tone that made it clear he was trying to make her feel ignorant for even questioning the lines and that she should trust him because, after all, he knew best.

"It's just concerning the sale of Mrs. Wilkins' property." He pointed to a line on the last page. "You see, you get nine hundred dollars just as we spoke about, one thousand, minus my ten percent fee."

It all seemed reasonable to Etta Jean, but didn't ring true to her. She couldn't shake off the feeling she was being taken in. But what was she to do, and who could she turn to? It seemed hopeless, so she decided to follow through with signing. She took up the pen and was just about to sign the papers when a hard knock came from the front door. Everyone looked across the room. When no one moved, a moment later there was another volley of knocks.

"Please, excuse me," Etta Jean said, placing the pen down and walking to the front door.

"Mr. Jaggers!" Etta Jean cried, taken completely by surprise.

He stood there smiling at her, again dressed finely and sporting a walking cane.

"Mrs. Newman, I hope I haven't come at an inopportune time?"

"No, not really, I was just in the middle of signing some legal papers...I'm selling some property for a friend."

"Then I came at the right time. Perhaps I can be of some help. May I come in?"

Etta Jean ushered Jaggers into the dining room and made the introductions.

"I didn't know, Mrs. Newman, that you had a lawyer," said Mr. Hagar, sounding overly friendly, which meant he was taken off guard.

"I've been away on business," Jaggers said. "But I'm back now, and I'll handle this."

Taking his time, he read the paper Etta Jean already signed.

"This looks to be a fine and straightforward document," Jaggers declared. "May I see the other papers, please?"

"They're just your normal bill of sale for the purchase of Mrs. Wilkins' property," Mr. Hagar said, sounding nervous.

"I'm sure they are," Jaggers said. "No reflection on you, sir, but I'd still like to have a look at them."

Jaggers took a long time in reading the document. They all sat waiting, uncomfortably silent. Finally, Jaggers placed the papers down, and all eyes were on him.

"I advise you not to sign this," Jaggers said, looking at Etta Jean. He pushed the papers across the table to Mr. Hagar. "I am sorry; sir, but my client will not be signing this, today or any other day."

"Why?" demanded Mr. Hagar. "It's just a bill of sale; and it's all very legal."

"I agree," Jaggers said. "It is all very legal, but it's not a very good deal. True, you are only taking ten percent for your work on this, but you've also put in many hidden fees which raise that ten percent up to nearly fifty percent. This makes me believe the amount being offered for the property is far greater than you've led my client to believe. From here on in, I will negotiate the sale for Mrs. Newman. We will keep the paper that gives her legal power over Mrs. Wilkins' property. I will have my office send you one hundred dollars for your help on that. Now, I advise you to take this trash, and you and your friend can leave. And just be thankful I don't take this to the courts and have you disbarred."

Mr. Hagar clearly understood he had been bested. He made no fuss and gave no argument. He took the papers, and he and his secretary left without a nod or a wink or a goodbye.

"As before, if you need me, I'm staying at the Parker House Hotel. I will start on negotiations to sell Mrs. Wilkins' property first thing tomorrow," Jaggers said as he stood up and headed for the front door.

"Mr. Jaggers, won't you stay for dinner?" Etta Jean asked.

"That's very kind of you; I'd like that. Besides, I have some matters to discuss with you," he looked at Mrs. Ford and Miriam, "and these other ladies, as well."

Since she did most of the cooking lately, Miriam volunteered to prepare the food, while Jaggers, Etta Jean, and Mrs. Ford sat talking in the parlor.

"Tell me, how far along are you in your reading of your mother's memories?" Jaggers asked Etta Jean. "What part are you on?"

"I'm at the part where she meets Duncan Monroe who hires her to travel to Colorado."

"Ah, yes, that is truly the beginning, when everything started."

"Everything…?"

"As for what I have to say to you and these other ladies, I'll explain over diner. I don't want to get ahead of myself. I want the young woman in the kitchen to hear what I have to say as well."

A half hour later, Jaggers and the three ladies sat at the dining table. He spoke to them as a friend might.

"I promised your mother to bring you along slowly. But with what has happened, your friend Mrs. Wilkins' misfortune, I feel we should move ahead."

None of the women understood what he meant. They sat silently waiting.

"Your mother became a wealthy woman in Colorado," he said to Etta Jean, "more wealthy than you can imagine, and she's left it all to you. She struggled all her last years to find her children. Despite all her money and influence, she was unsuccessful for years. Then when she learned of you, it was too late. She found you at the end of her life. Now, we can do this many ways."

He stopped for a moment to emphasize the seriousness of what he was about to say.

"Your mother's great wealth is yours to do as you please. You can ignore it, if you like, and I will see that it all goes to charity. But I doubt you will do that, though it is an option. Or you can sell her property, add the profits to her bank account, claim it for yourself, and live your life as you see fit. But might I suggest another scenario? Take up where your mother left off. Come to Colorado. Claim her dynasty. With my help, you can continue in her shoes. Either way, Mrs. Newman, you are richer than you ever dreamed possible. Think of it. You can give your daughter a magnificent life, and you can help your friend, Mrs. Wilkins, get the care she needs to recover. It's all yours for the asking."

Etta Jean didn't know what to say. Jaggers looked to Mrs. Ford and Miriam.

"I've checked on some things. It seems you have the ability to select good friends. I know, Mrs. Ford, that you are a widow with no family to speak of. It would be a blessing to all concerned, including you, to come to Colorado and continue Mrs. Wilkins' therapy." Then he looked to Miriam. "And you, young lady, I know you have no place to go. Come with us."

Etta Jean stopped him for a moment. "Let me understand this. You want us to move to Colorado. But, how...?"

"You still don't understand," he said with a chuckle. "You are a very wealthy woman. You have the money to do whatever you want. Your mother's house, I should say mansion, waits for you, as does all her property, investments, and bank account."

"What about Faye?" Etta Jean asked.

"We can travel by train. It will be difficult, but we can do it," he said. "Her life...all your lives will be better for it."

Etta Jean looked at the other two women. "What do you think?"

"It's your life," Mrs. Ford replied. "But if you want to go, I'll go, too."

"Count me in," Miriam added.

"Well, it looks like our lives are going to change," Etta Jean said.

"More than you'll ever know," Jaggers said, sounding very amused.

The three women look at each other and burst into a fit of laugher.

Etta Jean took hold of Jaggers' hand and shook it.

"Well, Mr. Jaggers, I guess were all game for an adventure."

"One more thing," Jaggers said, "from now on, you can all drop the 'Mister.' Just simple 'Jaggers' will do just fine."

Chapter XIII

Traveling West

It all sounded unbelievable, which worried Etta Jean. She knew the old saying that if it's too good to be true, it usually isn't good or true. But over the next few days, her concerns were put to rest. Jaggers had two thousand dollars deposited into Etta Jean's bank account for expenses. She was also told that if by chance she needed any more, it would be supplied. She had no idea how that could be possible. How could she ever need any more? It also made her wonder how large her mother's estate really was; it boggled her mind.

As well, Faye's property was sold within the week to the same investors who wanted to buy the property through Mr. Hagar. Only now, the price brought in was one thousand five hundred, as there were no hidden fees, and Jaggers dismissed the ten percent service fee.

Another week later, Etta Jean's home was sold for more than she would have ever dreamed to ask for. With a fully paid mortgage, it was all profit.

Everyone was excited, save for Liberty. The young girl was set in her ways and felt comfortable in the predictable repetition of her life. She would miss her friends from school, and all those she had made at church. Etta Jean did her best to ease the child's concerns, but only time would tell.

The problem on all their minds, which they knew they would have to face, was Faye. She'd shown such improvement but was far from well, and traveling was sure to be difficult.

A wheelchair was purchased; this would make it a little easier. But that was the least of their problems. She needed to be fed like a baby and cleaned up afterward as well. She needed to be sponge bathed every day, a massive chore in a home, in a bed. They could only image what it would be like traveling. It was complicated. And especially since she started eating solid foods again, hygiene would be a major problem. In reality, traveling on a train would be easier said than done.

They each took turns moving Faye in her wheelchair. It was clear it was too hard for the women to move her under some circumstances. Jaggers suggested hiring a male assistant. Etta Jean immediately knew who to ask.

It took only a few questions to the right people, and Etta Jean found where Morgan Young lived. Morgan, the handyman from the boarding house, though he was getting up in years, he was still spry and strong. Without the boarding house or a job, Morgan was quick to offer his service. There was no reason not to go to Colorado; he had nothing to tie him down.

It surprised Etta Jean that Regina Tuttle, the once-cook at the boarding house, was living with Morgan, or he was living with her – it wasn't quite clear. Etta Jean did not have the heart to offer Morgan a job with Regina standing there listening and not offer her one. Besides, Regina was a good worker and an excellent cook.

Etta Jean's first thought was to ask Jaggers if she could hire Regina as well. But then she realized it was her money, and if she were to continue with her mother's business, she should start taking responsibility for it. So she hired Regina as well. Jaggers did have something to say about it: he thought it was an excellent idea.

They went about packing what they needed for the journey. Other clothing and articles were crated and sent on ahead. Certain household items, such as kitchen utensils and furniture, Jaggers advised to leave for the new homeowners. Her mother's home, which she inherited, was well furnished. Instead, Etta Jean had Morgan drop these items at the church for those in need.

Finally, the day came to leave. Etta Jean locked up the house with a melancholy twist of the key and put it in the postbox.

They were all in their finest clothes. They'd dressed Faye and placed her in the wheelchair. Morgan took charge of wheeling her about. She was much thinner now, as thin as when she was a young girl, but she looked healthy. And when they arrived at the station, people stared as Morgan pushed her to the train. Some of the porters helped lift her and put her onboard.

They all road in a first-class compartment. Clearly this was the cause of much mumbling and pointing from many of the other passengers. A group of blacks traveling by rail was not uncommon, but to be in first-class was. It was then Etta Jean realized that money could erase many of the lines that were drawn to separate them from the world, but not from people's minds.

There was no direct train from Boston to Denver. They would have to make many stops and exchange trains several times. This was difficult. But Morgan proved his worth every time.

That first day was exciting: all of them looking out the window, and Liberty's nose pressed to the glass, watching the changing world pass by.

When lunchtime came, they worked their way to the dining car. They couldn't keep their eyes from the window-view of the world as it whipped by while they ate the most delicious foods.

"It's almost as good as mine," Regina admitted as she buttered her bread.

They were all having such a wonderful time, when a dark cloud descended. It was then Etta Jean realized that their presence was not appreciated, to put it mildly. Save for the waiters, they were the only black people in the car. Understand that this was a time when blacks could freely travel in that part of the country, but there were cars assigned for them, and sandwiches for sale were made available. A group of blacks traveling first-class and eating in the dining car wasn't the norm, and it was looked down on.

Etta Jean became aware of the stares from some the other passengers. These were not of curiosity, which she could understand. These were looks that could kill, if they were allowed. Some of the tables complained; others rose from their seats and stormed out, clearly angry. But there was nothing they could do; Jaggers saw to that. Money makes things happen. He'd paid a high price for their journey to be one of elegance and comfort.

It was so frustrating looking at the world through bars of prejudice. No matter how hard you try, there is always someone who won't listen or let you touch them. No amount of money can change the human heart.

Etta Jean learned over and whispered to Jaggers. "Is it possible for us to take our meals in our compartment from now on?"

Jaggers immediately knew what she implied. He was not unaware of the unfriendliness that filled the dining car. Many of the stares of hatred were directed at him as well for taking part in such a fiasco. He cupped his hand to whisper back to her.

"You can if you like. But let me tell you, your mother was strong. She would face and stand up to injustice wherever she found it. She always told me, 'Life may be safe hiding in a hole, but is it really a life?'"

"But what about Liberty...?" Etta Jean whispered back.

"You won't be there for all her life," he said. "It's like a muscle, the more you exercise it, the stronger it gets. I know it's rough, but imagine how strong she'll be if you start now. Talk to her; she's a smart child. Find out how she feels about it and hear what she has to say. She'll understand."

Etta Jean shook her head and wore a reluctant smile. "I can take it, if you can," she said, showing she was aware that some of the anger was directed at him, as well.

He smiled back, mostly impressed with her sensitivity and thoughtfulness.

****

The railways to Denver were many; there were multiple stops in as many cities. The train schedules didn't always line up, so sometimes the stops were as long as two or three days.

Each city they stayed in was a new experience. They stayed at the best hotels, shopped at the finest stores, and ate at the best restaurants. It was clear this was done under protest and disapproval by many around them, but money changes everything. Etta Jean was sure Jaggers was paying more than the going rate for much of what they did and purchased, sometimes twice as much. But Jaggers insisted they could afford it, and he was making sure their travels were as good experience as possible.

Still there were times in certain cities where their money was no good. The hotels and restaurants would not serve them at any price. On those occasions, they stayed in the best hotel they could find in the black part of town. And they ate at black restaurants, as well. Though she never voiced it, Etta Jean felt inward satisfaction as to the way her people treated Jaggers. There were stares, which were understandable, what with a white man in the black part of town. But never was there any animosity shown to him. This made Etta Jean beam with pride for her people.

Traveling with Faye was not easy. But strangely, her awareness seemed to perk up. It was as if the stimulation of traveling was good for her. Her eyes gleamed with new life, and her speech was no longer grunts but clear sounds that were obvious attempts to speak. Not exact or definite words, mind you, but syllables that were apparent. This made her friends hopeful of her recovery.

As for Liberty, she took to it all like a duck to water. She was excited and happy, which made her mother feel better about her decisions. Etta Jean hoped the excitement of a new life would help her daughter forget the old and adjust easily.

****

Finally, they came to the last leg of their journey, Colorado. They stared out the windows, awestruck. They'd never seen such beauty: high snowcapped mountains; deep green valleys; swift, white-water flowing rivers; lakes like giant mirrors; and sunrises and sunsets no artist could every truly capture. Boston had its charm, but natural beauty such as this filled them with awe. It was at this point they relaxed, and the fear that they all may have made a mistake in moving was beginning to disappear.

Denver is large and highly populated with much coming and going. But unlike Boston, it is spread out and airy with the mountains all around kissing the blue sky and inhibiting billowy white clouds as they race from west to east. It wasn't like the city parks they were used to. It wasn't a bit of nature in the city; it was a bit of civilization in the midst of nature.

At the station, they waited for their luggage, which had increased due to all their new purchases. A carriage and a flatbed buggy pulled up. Two men began loading their luggage onto the buggy. Jaggers opened the door of the carriage.

"This is our transportation to Walker Manor, just a few miles from the edge of town." He turned to Etta Jean who was watching the two men loading the buggy. He moved in close and whispered to her. "Smile; it's good for management and employee relationships. These two men work for you." She looked at him in surprise. "Two of many..." he concluded.

Etta Jean nodded and smiled at the men; they nodded and smiled back.

It took a while to get Faye into the carriage. The two men helped Morgan get her off the train and into the buggy. They put her wheelchair in the back of the flatbed with the luggage.

Riding through town, Etta Jean could not help but feel the difference of Denver over Boston. Blacks walked about freely in Boston, but there was an air of separatism. Denver was different; people came and went without care of anything other than their own business. Blacks not only moved about freely, they went about unnoticed. Some looked poor and dressed shabby, while others seemed prosperous and well-dressed, and none of it seemed to matter.

Once they drove out to the edge of town, they passed miles of fields, forests, hills, valleys, streams, and lakes, all under that great blue sky.

"It's so beautiful here," Etta Jean commented.

"I'm glad you like it," Jaggers remarked. "It's all yours."

Etta Jean looked at him inquisitively.

"All along this four-mile road from town to the Walker Manor is yours, as well as four hundred acres beyond the house," he added.

They drove up to a tall iron gate and through a grand gateway, reminiscent of the plantations down south, as was the two-story mansion they drove up to, a quarter mile from the gate.

Holding Liberty's hand, Etta Jean got out of the carriage and stood in awe of the greatness of their new home.

"I can't believe this," Etta Jean said.

"Believe it," Jaggers said.

The others got out of the carriage and stood next to Etta Jean, all amazed at the size and grandeur of the home.

Before unloading the luggage from the buggy, the two men took down the wheelchair from the flatbed, and then helped Morgan get Faye out of the carriage and into the chair. Morgan wheeled her to where the others stood.

Etta Jean bent low and placed her hand on Faye's shoulder. "What do you think, Faye? This is going to be our new home."

They all turned to look at the woman. And as marvelous as the new home was, it did not compare to the look on Faye's face. There was no question about it, the woman was smiling.

Chapter XIV

A Hard Road

Moving over a hundred men and the supplies needed to care for them across thousands of miles is a long and slow journey. It was impossible to carry enough food and water for everyone in one large wagon. Water was not too difficult as there were many streams and creeks along the way, but food was another story. We had to stop at different cities to buy more goods. Often, we went miles out of our way to get to these cities. This slowed us down all the more.

There was another obstacle in our way, a little thing called "The Civil War." A fair amount of the men with us were free black men. The other and larger amount were white men from foreign countries. These foreigners did not take sides with the North or the South. Often we heard shots off in the distance. We always went out of our way to avoid battles. This, too, slowed us down.

When confronted with the Confederate troops, the commanding officer would demand that all able-bodied men sign up. Duncan paid off many a demanding general to let us go unmolested. Payment was always in the way of food. And these generals would not hear the offer of any amount of food – they took it all.

It was the same with the Union troops. They would take all our provisions in exchange for safe passage.

Duncan solved this problem. The next town we came to, he purchased another wagon and filled it only halfway with food and provisions. The original wagon was filled with food we would be preparing. When stopped by Rebels or Yankees, we offered them what they thought to be everything we had, but it was the half-filled wagon. This saved us time and money.

It was a difficult life, preparing food for so many folks every day. We were up hours before the others. Breakfast was usually coffee, biscuits, and bacon. And there were mountains of beans served with every meal. Evening meal wasn't much different: beans with salt pork, or dried beef served with more biscuits and coffee. After we purchased food in a city, we always had a good supply of potatoes and onions, which we threw into the mix as long as they remained fresh. Now and then, some of the scouts who rode ahead on horseback would shoot something for the pot.

Once a week, we'd camp for a full day. This would allow everyone, including the horses, to rest and get their strength and spirits up. We'd always camp by a river or stream for many reasons. We'd be able to replenish our water supply. Some of the men would fish, which was a nice change in the menu. Others would hunt wild game. And lastly, we would be able to wash the clothes the men wore the past week. So, as the horses rested, we still had a job to do.

Though we did our best to avoid the war, we still came across fresh battlefields from battles fought anywhere from hours to many days ago. Duncan could not ignore these sites filled with dead soldiers. We'd stop and bury the dead, if there were only a few. If the number was much greater, we'd put them in a pile, North and South together, and start a funeral pyre. We would stay the night and keep fueling the fire till the bodies were ash. Of course, this slowed us down. But I had to respect Duncan for doing it, and I must admit I agreed with him.

He also earned my respect whenever we camped on the outskirts of towns. Duncan would allow the men to go into town and do whatever they cared to do. But he never allowed it in his camp. No working ladies were let into camp; in town was fine, but not in camp. As well, drunkenness in town was one thing, but not in his camp. And if a man got drunk and passed out in town, we were most likely gone when he woke up. We left many a man behind to fend for himself and catch up with us days later.

On more than one occasion, Christina expressed how she felt Duncan was sweet on me. The first time she said it, I laughed. Every time after, I ignored it and never entertained the thought of it being possible. When Duncan began coming to our wagon every night to check on us, I assumed it was no more than good business sense. He was being responsible, checking on his people. And when he began to ride to the back of the line to where we were to check on us, still I thought nothing of it. But when his nightly visits became longer, it made me wonder if Christina was seeing something I wasn't. He'd pour a cup of coffee and sit with me next to the fire. He'd ask me all sorts of questions about me and told me about him. It was all very friendly and enjoyable, but I had to question his motives.

It made me feel uncomfortable inside, and worried. Christina's words took root in my mind and played over and over. To be honest, it scared me. Duncan was charming; there was no doubt about that. And the feelings I held for him were growing stronger. If he only thought of us as friends, it would break my heart. And if he was serious, what could we do about? I was not going to be any man's mistress. It bothered me so that I became short with him, against what my heart was telling me. When he came around, I politely told him I was too busy to stop and talk, and then went off to find something to busy myself with. I felt bad for doing this and was not sure if it was the right thing. Duncan still continued to check on us twice a day. This confused me even more for it meant he really wasn't interested in me and was just doing his job. Or it could have meant that he was not a man to give up easily. It is so interesting how strangely a person thinks once the heart has its say.

* * * * * * * *

The farther northwest we traveled, the more we left the war behind, which was a good thing. But the weather was changing. Winter set in. First, the trees turned into rainbows of colors, and then the leaves fell to the ground, exposing the naked branches. The wind blew through the camp like a sharp knife, leaving my face and hands burning. Then it happened, a small indication of what was coming. First, a frost appeared on the ground in the early morning, and then a frost covered the ground and stayed the whole day through. Finally, the snows came.

There is a saying among the Indians of America, "Big snow, little snow; small snow, big snow."

That's how it was. At first, the snowflakes were large like beautiful lace doilies floating to the ground. These would melt as soon as they touched the earth. But then, small flurries came down. These would stick to everything. And before you knew it, the world was a white canvas with no color. Then the snows came in inches and then in feet, till it was impossible to move forward.

We camped in a valley near a lake. We did what we could to stay warm and stay alive. Then all hell broke loose.

With the snows came the fever. Men fell where they stood, unable to move. We were caught in a place and time where nothing else mattered. We covered those with the fever with blankets and did our best to keep them warm. The numbers grew everyday till there was no way we could take care of all of them.

We did our best, but there was nothing we could do. Dozens died and we buried them. All we could do was pray over them and their graves. Finally, as if they were one person, the fevers broke. We were left with many well, but weakened men. We fed and nursed them back to health, but many had been lost. There is a field somewhere in the northwest with thirty unmarked graves where the grass has grown and covered up the memories of hopeful men.

* * * * * * * *

At first look, Denver seemed to be no more than a northern version of Brent Creek in a much more glorious setting. There was not much to the city when I first arrived – only one main street with the usual buildings of commerce every small town has, and around it another city consisting of tents and more tents.

But there was an air of hopefulness that you rarely find anywhere else. Here were thousands of people who'd gambled everything in hopes of having a better life.

We set up camp some three miles from the center of town. This was the property owned by Duncan where he planned to dig for gold. It would be a long, hard process, but if the vein was as rich as he suspected, the sky was the limit.

Tents were set up for the men. My workers and I were given tents to live in, and there was a large tent to prepare and serve food. Only now, things were different. Duncan provided his men only one meal a day at midday for a lunch break. When the men started to receive wages, that's when we started to prepare food for sale. The men had only three options: cook their own food, which some did; go into town where the one and only restaurant served good but expensive food; or buy their meals from us.

I was surprised Duncan never demanded a cut. After all, it was on his property, in his tents, and with his equipment. But all he demanded was that the meals we sold were made from supplies we'd purchased and not his. This was only fair.

It wasn't long before I had more money than I could hide in my tent. I went into town and opened an account at the only bank. It became a weekly ritual to go to town and make a deposit.

As well as serving meals, I started the laundry service again. I also offered haircuts and tooth pulling. The men were not very interested in their appearances, but this did pull in a fair amount of money.

We lost many men who set off to try their luck at gold mining in the mountains on their own. But for every man we lost, two would show up to work for Duncan with the promise of a good wage. With the inflow of men, I had to take on more workers, mostly blacks and Chinese from the town.

As expected, the men went into town on Saturday nights to kick up their heels. That's when we made the most money on laundry and haircuts. That evening meal was smaller as most eyes were set on a meal at the town's restaurant.

Months later, they'd dig a large, proper mine in the side of the mountain, and it was paying off well, far beyond Duncan's expectations. But he was not one to be satisfied with just sitting back. He was always thinking.

Duncan came to me one day. "I've decided to open up another camp on the other side of the mountain and start mining there as well. I was hoping you'd offer your services there. Do you think you could set that up?"

I told him I would. It would mean more workers, but that was no problem. It would also mean I'd double my income. That's when I questioned Duncan's motives.

"Why are you so good to me?" I asked.

He smiled awkwardly, as if the question made him uncomfortable.

He came back with, "Well, you do a good job."

We both knew that was not the answer.

I repeated my question. "Why are you so good to me?"

The smile left his face and he looked at me so seriously. "It's because I…"

He stopped midsentence, turned, and left.

Chapter XV

Familiar Smells

Life is full of change, which is one of the reasons life is so difficult. Etta Jean was not prepared for such changes.

Liberty had no problem adjusting to her new life. To her it was a great adventure. Many of the workers and servants on the property – blacks and whites – lived onsite and had families with children her age. In no time, she was romping and playing with the other children. Etta Jean had always raised her daughter to feel secure, and now Liberty was so happy.

As for Miriam, Regina, and Morgan, they were pleased with their rooms and position in life. They went about doing what they'd always done, working in the kitchen and in the garden, but now for higher pay and in a more relaxed atmosphere. They couldn't ask for more.

Mrs. Ford roomed next to Faye. Both their rooms were large and luxurious, located in the back of the house and overlooking the garden by the large pond. Often, Mrs. Ford would wheel Faye through the garden and around the pond. Mrs. Ford increased the hours of therapy as Faye improved. She began moving her head about and lifting her arms. Her eyes were full of life, and she often smiled. And the sounds she uttered were beginning to sound less like grunts and more like words.

But Etta Jean did not adjust as well as the others. Jaggers, who came to the house every day, noticed this and took to helping her as best he could. Over tea in the library, they talked.

"I'm not my mother!" Etta Jean insisted.

"No one's expecting you to be," Jaggers answered.

"No? Then why am I here? I'm not a businesswoman. I'm not used to bossing people around."

"Your mother never bossed anyone around," Jaggers pointed out. "I can tell you haven't read enough of your mother's diary to understand. Everyone liked her. She offered people jobs for a good wage. And she never bossed anyone around. 'Please' and 'thank you,' was always part of any request she made. And those who worked for her would do anything she asked because they trusted her and respected her. You can be that type of woman and still be who you are. There's no need to be your mother or anyone else."

"I just don't know where to start," Etta Jean said.

Jaggers smiled. "Why don't you and I take the day to see what it is that you've inherited? Maybe then you'll know where to start. I'll be by tomorrow to get you after breakfast."

****

Early the next morning, Etta Jean was too lost in thought to eat. She drank her coffee as she happily watched Liberty eat her fill. One of the workers told her Jaggers was waiting outside for her. True to his word, Jaggers sat in a two-seat buggy.

"Good morning, Mrs. Newman. Are you ready?"

"As ready as I will ever be, I guess." Etta Jean said as she hopped up in the seat next to him.

The first part of their journey took them toward town. The road was the same they had traveled the day they first arrived.

"Now, you say I own all this property?" Etta Jean asked, looking from left to right.

"It's all yours," Jaggers said.

There were plowed rows of the strangest plants being tended to by workers.

"These crops," Etta Jean said, "I don't recognize them. What are they?"

"Herbs, flowers, medicinal plants," Jaggers replied.

"I don't understand," Etta Jean questioned.

"By the end of the day, it will all make sense, I promise," Jaggers reassured her.

In town, Jaggers tied the one-horse buggy on Main Street.

"Do I own property in town?" Etta Jean asked.

"Not one square inch," Jaggers answered.

"Then why are we here?"

"I want to show something that may help you understand your mother better," he said.

The first shop they went into was Smith's Dry Goods, a small shop that from the activity was doing a fair amount of business.

As they entered the shop, Jaggers leaned over and whispered in her ear, "They're real name is *Schmidt*, German style. They thought Smith would sound more American."

Inside, Etta Jean looked around. The shop was small but filled with whatever merchandise a self-sufficient person could not provide for themselves. A small, gray-haired old woman approached them. She had a deep, strong German accent.

"Mr. Jaggers, so good to see you, how may we help you?"

Jaggers pointed to Etta Jean. "This is Mrs. Newman, Elizabeth Walker's daughter."

The women went into a frenzy, shouting, "Hans, come quick, come quick."

A small, gray-haired man rushed to her side. "What is it, *meine liebste?*"

"This here is Mrs. Walker's daughter."

"Oh, how can we be of service?" asked Hans.

"We just wanted to say hello," Jaggers said.

"You like sweets, *ja?*" asked the woman. She went to the counter, took up a small paper bag, and filled it with candy from a jar. "Here you are. Whatever we can do, just let us know," the woman pleaded.

Etta Jean thanked them, and she and Jaggers left.

"I don't understand," Etta Jean said.

"You will," Jaggers said.

Next, they entered one of the three restaurants in town, Holliman's.

As soon as they entered, a young man of thirty ran to greet them.

"Mr. Jaggers, what a pleasant surprise. How can I help you?" the young man asked, wearing a large smile.

"Just some coffee and eggs," Jaggers replied. "This is Mrs. Newman, Elizabeth Walker's daughter."

"Then the very best," he said as he guided them to a table.

"It's all very good," Etta Jean said as she ate her breakfast.

"I'm glad you like it," said the young man. "Come in anytime. You and your family can eat anytime for free."

"That's very kind of you, Mr. Holliman," Etta Jean said.

"My pleasure," said the young man as he walked away.

"I still don't understand," Etta Jean said outside as they got back on the buggy.

"Your mother believed in this town; she also believed in people. When she came into money, she started to lend people money to start their own businesses. She was very careful who she lent money to. But for those she did lend to, the interest was lower than the bank. She made a lot of money this way, but she also made a lot of friends, too. This town wouldn't be what it is today if it wasn't for your mother."

Next, they rode about a mile south from town. They came to a large building. There was no mistaking what it was. It was a lumberyard with wood in various degrees of transformation from trees to planks. Inside, it was hard to talk or think over the dim of the buzz saws. A tall, gray-haired black man came to them smiling. They had to shout to be heard.

"This is Mr. Tom Dunsany; he's the manager here. He's been running the yard since your mother opened it." He shook Tom's hand. "Tom, this is Mrs. Newman, Mrs. Walker's daughter – your new boss."

"Why don't we go into my office?" he shouted. They followed him into a small room with a single desk. When he shut the door, the noise was cut in half. "It's a pleasure to meet you, Mrs. Newman."

"Why don't you explain what you do here, Tom," Jaggers suggested.

"It's simple. Your mother looked out one day and said, 'We sure got a lot of trees here,' and that was the beginning. We have jacks cutting trees in the mountain, and there's a team that hauls them down here where we slice them up into lumber. We take 'em down to the railway and ship the planks all over the country. It's hard work, but it's really that simple."

"Tom's the best there is," Jaggers announced.

"Thank you for your hard work," Etta Jean said.

"Thank you, ma'am. Drop by anytime. Now, if you can excuse me, I got to see to some matters."

"Don't let us keep you," Jaggers said.

Outside as they rode away, Jaggers declared, "He's a good man, that Tom." They got back on the road going north. "Now for the big surprise," Jaggers said, laughing.

Two miles down the road, they came to a large one-story building with many windows, many doors, and loading docks on both ends. It could only be described as an oversized warehouse.

Jaggers stopped the buggy and helped Etta Jean down. "Now you're going to find out what all those fields were growing. This was your mother's biggest moneymaker."

As they approached the building, Etta Jean's nose caught the scent of something very familiar. It was a complicated smell – a mixture of sweet, fragrant, floral, pungent, burned wood, pine, and eucalypti – and very familiar.

The main door in the center of the building opened and out stepped an elderly black woman, smiling as she walked toward them.

"This is Felicia Mansfield. She's been with the company from its inception by your mother. Felicia, this is Mrs. Newman, your new boss."

The two women shook hands. Felicia was a tiny, frail woman with the smoothest of skin and dark, shiny hair. In some ways she looked elderly, but still there was a youthfulness glowing from her. One look into her eyes told you volumes: this was a woman of great character and wisdom.

"Your mother and I go back many years. We were good friends, and I knew her well. She was a great lady. You should be proud."

Etta Jean didn't know how to respond, so she said nothing.

"Well, why don't we take a tour of the factory?" Felicia said.

"Wait...factory? What do you make here?" Etta Jean asked.

"Why, don't you know?" Felicia smiled. "It was your mother's idea. They're all her recipes. We manufacture..."

"Don't tell her," Jaggers interrupted. "Let's see if she can guess."

"Oh, that's cruel," Felicia laughed.

"No, that's all right," Etta Jean said, smiling. "I'm willing to play along."

"Well, if that's the case, we should enter the building at the loading dock on the far left side of the building," Felicia said, pointing.

They walked up the stairs of the dock.

Felicia started the tour. "This is where we unload the ingredients we use. Some of them we grow ourselves; others are brought in by train. But I'd say we grow ninety percent of what we need.

She turned and opened a large sliding door. They entered the building.

"This is where we store the ingredients. These two ladies are in charge of storing everything in its place and keeping a record of everything that comes in and goes out into the factory," Felicia said, pointing to the two workers and the shelves and bins.

The familiar smell was even more potent in the building.

"I know this smell. I've smelled it before," Etta Jean said, taking in deep breaths.

Felicia laughed. "I know you do. And I'm sure the smell of our products will give us away before you see what we make. Let's step into the next room."

Jaggers was smiling, enjoying this guessing game.

In the next room, workers crushed the plants and boiled them in water, slowly extracting the goodness from them.

"There's that smell again," Etta Jean declared.

Felicia just smiled at Jaggers as the two shared the secret, knowing it would not be long before Etta Jean was in on it.

The room after that, workers filled large vats with the plant essence and other ingredients such as oils and creams.

Etta Jean walked to one of the vats and took in a deep breath. "Hair cream…" she shouted. She went to another vat and breathed in. "Skin cream…" she proclaimed. "You make beauty products for black women!"

Felicia laughed out loud. "I told you that your nose would figure it out."

They walked to the far end of the large room where workers scooped the finished products out of the vats and filled jars with the lotions and potions. At a table against the far wall, a group of women glued labels onto the jars. Etta Jean picked up a jar and read the label.

"'Dark and Beautiful'…! You're telling me my mother owned Dark and Beautiful beauty products for black women? I've been using these products for years and never knew."

She looked at the label closer and noticed some small print she never paid much attention to – "Made in Denver, Colorado."

"Your mother not only owned the company, she started it from the ground up," said Felicia. "All the recipes are hers. Once she got the factory started, she taught me how to run it and put me in charge. And I've been running it ever since."

Entering the next room, Felicia gestured at stacks of crates.

"And here's where we pack and store the finished product. It goes out onto that loading dock; then it's put on the trains and distributed to different markets across the country," Felicia finished the tour with an air of great and well-deserved pride.

On the ride back home, Etta Jean's mind was full of questions, and Jaggers knew it.

"It seems you have two choices," he said. "As you can see, everything you inherited from your mother pretty much runs itself. You can just sit back and live like a queen, or you can get your hands dirty and dig right in. Get involved."

"Like my mother?" Etta Jean asked.

"It's not a bad life. Think of it as an adventure. Who knows where it will lead you?" he said.

"What about you?" Etta Jean asked with a hint of suspicion.

"What about me? I was your mother's lawyer, and she was my only client."

Etta Jean shook her head. "Maybe so, but there's more to it than that, I can feel it. You know so much about everything to do with my mother. There's something you're not telling me."

"I'm not hiding anything," Jaggers laughed. "You just need to read further into your mother's diary. It's all there."

That evening after checking on Liberty and Faye, Etta Jean went to her room. She lit the lamp next to her bed, got in, and tilted the notebook toward the light.

Chapter XVI

Apply and Rinse

Over the next few years, everything changed. We went from living and working in tents to shacks, which was fine for a while. The town was changing, too. The population grew; first it doubled, and then tripled. On the outskirts of town, people built shacks and cabins. But within the immediate township, houses were being erected.

This was mostly a good thing. This meant more families, schools, banks, churches, prosperity, and culture. Civilization had come to Denver. But with all these positive things came also the negative. With it came prejudice and segregation.

A fine line separated the peoples, an invisible line on the map, but as real as any canyon. There were the whites, the blacks, and the Chinese. Happily, there was no animosity between these cultures; in fact, there was a clear respect for one another. But there was no crossing that line.

No one had to tell us how the Civil War was going; we saw the results every day. More and more worn and undernourished white men straggled into town looking for work and a new life. All their accents were southern accents. In this way, we knew the South was losing the war.

It got so bad that at one point the Confederates sent a small troop of soldiers to weed out the deserters. They rode into town – there must have been twenty of them – and stayed for two weeks. I don't believe they caught one deserter.

It seems the town was split on what action to take. It wasn't safe for these runaways to seek refuge in the white part of town. Some whites sided with the South and would have given them up in a heartbeat. While some whites sided with the North and would have hidden them, how do you identify a Northern sympathizer from a Southern one?

The Chinese citizens couldn't care less. Though some would hide a Johnny Reb for a price, there were many who would turn them in for a reward. No, it was not wise to go to the Chinese.

There was only one place in town. Every black sided with the North, and one less Johnny Reb in uniform was one day closer to a Northern victory.

Love and war can lead to the strangest of bedfellows. For two weeks these runaway Johnny Rebs hid in the homes of black folk. They slept, ate, and lived with black folk.

When the investigating Confederates gave up and left, these Johnny Rebs came out of hiding. And don't think it didn't change them deeply, because it did. I got to know some of these men. Many of them left after the war, but others sent for their families and made a new life for themselves in Denver. These were changed men. And for these men, the color line disappeared. It was a good thing.

When the war ended, a flood of people came, doubling our population in three months. We were the well-known boomtown. There was gold, lumber, and industry. People were becoming rich, and the allure drew folks like iron to a magnet. The South had its troubles after the war. The North was what it was and had always been. For the adventurous spirit and the entrepreneur there were only three destinations: Texas, California, or Colorado. There were fortunes to be made in Texas, but only with hard work in unbearable heat. There were plenty of opportunities in California, but the competition was the greatest there. If you didn't mind long, cold winters, Colorado was the perfect choice.

My relationship with Duncan grew into the finest and closest of friendships. If Christina's suspicions were true, he never let on; though in the back of my mind I wished it were so. But I'd lived enough of life to know that it does what it wants, and only rarely do you and it agree.

I'd saved enough money to move on from my one-room shack. I bought a small one-bedroom house in the black section of town. I asked Christina if she'd like to move in, but she was happy on her own. Minnie and Teresa were as cozy as two bugs in a rug in their little shack. So I was on my own.

I made many friends quickly. I joined the church, the black church, of course. Before long, word got out that I was a midwife. With the town growing, there was great call for midwives. Surprisingly, I was even called to the homes of some of the folks in the white part of town, though I never once had a Chinese customer.

Many a night, I went without sleep helping to bring a child into the world. I didn't need the money. Often, if I knew the family to be needy, I didn't charge them a cent. Many a cake and pie were left on my doorstep.

It was a bittersweet ministry I'd taken up. On one hand, helping folks and seeing new life come into the world was a joy and a blessing. But it made me think of my children. Sadly, I was beginning to forget what they looked like. Not that it matter much. So much time had passed that I probably wouldn't recognize them if we walked by each other on the street. I tried not to think about it or too often, or I'd start crying. Still, I always held hope I'd see them again.

Two nights before Christmas, I got a knock on my door. It was Albert Haze. Seemed his wife, Tina, who'd been expecting, well, their child just was so excited about Christmas he wasn't going to wait. Albert was as nervous as a chicken in a hot pot. I got my things and followed him to his place.

Tina was in bed in misery and hurting real bad. It was her first child, and they can be the hardest. She was young, that was on her side. But there's no telling sometimes.

I placed my hands on her belly. Don't ask me exactly how I knew, but after delivering so many babies, I knew this was going to be a long night.

I had Albert put the kettle on. I put some Wormwood in a cup, filled it with hot water and let it seep till it was a dark and bitter tea. I had a hard time getting Tina to drink it, but it helped. Twenty minutes later, the pain diminished.

By midnight, we were no more along than when I had arrived three hours earlier. I don't know what it is, but most children like coming into this world in the late night or the darkest hours of the morning. It was four in the morning and still dark when Tina went into it like a bull trying to fit in a broom closet: a lot of grunting, sweating, and wheezing. Once a child comes to its time, nothing in the world can stop it. Five minutes after four, I was holding a fine baby boy, crying to beat the band.

Once I got the child cleaned up, I put him in his mother's arms. Albert stood bedside, grinning from ear to ear. Tina held him as long as she could and then she fell asleep; thankfully, the baby did, too. I put the baby into the new crib already waiting for its first occupant. I told Albert to go into the parlor and get some sleep. It had been a difficult birth, so just to be on the safe side I sat in a chair next to the bed and dozed off.

As the first ray of morning light came through the window, we were all wakened by a very hungry young man. As Tina nursed him, I got a good look at her. She was worse for the wear, but there was more. As any woman will tell you, having a baby is hard on the body, at any age, even after the birth. Sometimes strange things happen. I looked at her scalp. She'd lost clumps of hair, and the skin was dry and discolored.

"Do ya think it'll come back?" Tina asked when she noticed I was looking at the top of her head.

"There's no reason to believe it won't. Tell you what, when I was growing up, I learned lots about natural herbs for hair and skin care. I'll come by tomorrow with something that might help."

I turned to leave and found Albert standing in the bedroom doorway.

"We don't know how to thank you, Miss Elizabeth. We'll pay ya when we can. I promise."

"It's all right," I told them, but they had their pride.

"We'd name the baby after you, if it were girl," Tina said.

I told them it didn't matter. They named the child Richard after my late husband. I thought it was a nice gesture, and I was sure if Richard were looking down, it made him smile.

I went home, exhausted. I stopped by the camp and did some work, but I don't think I was much help. I went home that night. I was so tired I fell asleep in my easy chair and didn't wake until early the next morning.

The sunlight was just coming over the horizon when I went out to the fields beyond the town. I knew what to look for, so it didn't take me long. I'd learned about such things as a young slave girl, and thankfully it was something I never forgot. I went home with an armful of plants. I extracted the goodness from them and mix it with some cooking oil, the only base I had available.

I went to see Tina. She was looking tired, but she and the baby were doing well. I applied the mixture to her scalp and massaged it in. Then I took a warm towel and wrapped it around her head.

"Now, I want you to keep it in all day and then wash it out tonight. Tomorrow, you do the same. You rub some into your scalp and wrap your head with a warm towel. Do that every day for a week. Then do it every other day for another week. And then twice a week for two weeks; after that, only once a week. Let me know if it helps or if you have any questions. If you have any trouble with the baby, you have Albert come and get me, you understand?" I told her. She looked a bit put out by the towel, but she was willing to try anything.

Life went on as usual. I was busy with my work. I hadn't heard from Albert and Tina, so I assumed everything was fine. After a month's time, we were well into the New Year, and they were the last people on my mind.

It was the last Sunday of January, and Christina and I attended church. Just before service started, in walked Tina and Albert. She was holding their newborn son, Richard, in her arms as they paraded up to the front of the church, proud as peacocks. And rightfully so; little Richard was a fine-looking child. Albert was all smiles, nodding his head as they passed the congregation. Tina was looking well wearing her Sunday best.

Quite a lot of women in the church like to wear a stylish hat to church. It's not a must-do, but it is the fashion. Still, many of the younger ladies didn't wear a hat, or for that matter, could afford one. Tina was not wearing a hat.

It wasn't only noticeable to me, but to everyone else – I should say, every woman – in church that day. Most of Tina's hair had returned, her scalp was smooth and clear, and her hair was dark, shiny, and healthy looking.

After service, I met with Tina outside. It was difficult getting to her. Everyone wanted to see the baby, and just as many wanted to know the story behind Tina's near-full head of hair.

"Here she is! Here's the woman who saved my baby and my hair," Tina shouted, pointing at me.

It was true. Up close, I saw the difference. Her hair and scalp had improved one hundred percent.

"That stuff really worked," she told me, but others were listening in. "And ya know what? Couple of days of applying it to my head, I noticed my hands were getting smoother. So I'd rub my hands with it, and you wouldn't believe the difference. So, I started rubbing it all over – my arms, my neck, and even my face. In no time, my skin looked better than ever. It's a miracle, I tell ya, a miracle. Simply a hair and skin miracle."

I guess I don't have to tell you what happened next. Every woman at church, and eventually every black woman in town, wanted some of my concoction. I had to say no. I didn't have the time to start making batches for every gal in town. But they kept at me.

Then I thought if I'm going to do this, then let's do it. Every day, after work, I asked many of my workers to come to my house where we worked into the night making small batches of my concoction. I paid them well, hoping to make it all back in sales. We'd collect the wild plants until sundown, and then we'd cook them down and have them mixed by early morning. I isolated the formula into two recipes, one for hair and one for skin. This way, we'd have two separate and different products.

It was an exhausting enterprise, working through the night, getting little sleep, and rising at the crack of dawn to put in a full day in the camp. But it didn't take long to realize it was worth it. We were selling faster than we could make it. I doubled everyone's wages. I had women knocking on my door day and night, either looking for work or wanting to buy the hair and skin products, or both.

I came to two revelations. I realized that selling only in one town was just the tip of the iceberg. I also realized there was no reason I needed to be so hands-on. I needed someone to run this new business for me. That's when I thought of Felicia Mansfield, a widow with no children. She was close to my age with strong character and work ethics. She'd worked for me ever since her husband died two years earlier in December from pneumonia. I knew instinctively she should be the one I chose to run my new business, not only because I liked and respected her, but because she was one of the sharpest women I knew.

After explaining what I expected of her, Felicia jumped at the chance. She'd run the business as I did out of my home. She put together a small crew, and in a week we were in production.

I took all my savings out of my bank account. When Duncan heard what I was up to, he asked if he could invest in my new venture. Not that he believed in it, he just didn't want me to go belly-up if things went bad. I told him I wanted to do this on my own. He told me if it didn't work out, he'd always back me with money. I thought this was a sweet gesture, but there was no call for that. I was confident I'd succeed.

One night over coffee, Teresa, Minnie, Felicia, and I sat around my breakfast table trying to think up a name for this stuff. We came up with some real lulus, but in the end we decided to call it, "Dark and Beautiful." I thought it was a good choice. It pretty much said it all.

Christina drew the artwork for the labels and I must say it came out well. I sent off for labels and five hundred small, empty jars from Cincinnati. We got them a week later and began to fill them.

Through the post, I contacted stores in black neighborhoods in cities close by They couldn't resist the deal I gave them. If they took fifty jars of Dark and Beautiful, twenty-five skin cream and twenty-five hair cream, I'd guarantee them that it all would sell. If all fifty jars didn't sell within two months, I'd buy back the unsold jars at full price, at the store's selling price. It was a win-win for them.

My strategy was simple. Tina Haze was my ace in the hole. Whenever we put our product in a new store, in a new city, Tina would travel to that city. I'd pay all her traveling and lodging expenses, as well as pay her handsomely for her time. Meanwhile, Albert would stay home with the baby.

Tina would travel to the new city. There she'd speak to black women's groups, church groups, and women's clubs. Wherever black women gathered, Tina would give her testimony, of which her lovely hair and skin were the most impressive. We went into a new store in a new city every two weeks. Eventually, we branched out to stores in other states.

I ran the special offer to stores for the first year till Dark and Beautiful was a well-know, proven, and demanded product. In all that time, not once did I buy any jars back. The first order jars usually sold within the first month.

In the second year, I took half my earnings and bought a warehouse outside of town, which became the headquarters of Dark and Beautiful. It was a great success.

Strange as it may sound, I believe Duncan was disappointed. Not that he was jealous or that he didn't want the best for me. I think perhaps he would have liked to see me fail only so he could come to my rescue.

When I fully came to this realization, I understood that Christina's words were always true. We had a good friendship, but there was an underlying current of emotion that needed to come to the surface. I decided if he wasn't going to make the first move, I would.

Chapter XVII

In Good Hands

Dark and Beautiful became successful beyond all my dreams. I learned that one of the keys to success is to take care of those who helped you get there, and I took care of all my people very well. Not just in wages, but in encouragement. People appreciate being appreciated. And when you take time to know them and understand their needs, you make a connection. You make a friend, and a friend will do almost anything for a friend.

Money makes money so I began to seek other avenues to make more. One morning, I looked out on the mountain view and realized the amount of trees around us was staggering. Sure, the buildings of the town were all built with local timber. And sure, there were more than two successful lumberyards in and around town. But none of them came close to what I had in mind. I figured, if I could ship hair and skin products around the country, I could ship lumber.

I bought some heavily wooded areas and built a saw mill on the same property. Like my beauty line, I put someone else, someone with knowledge and talent, in charge and paid them well. Through Duncan, I met Tom Dunsany, a man who'd lived most his life in Canada in the lumber business. He'd come like so many others to Colorado to make his fortune; and like so many others, he had failed miserably. But I saw he still had potential. Tom set up a camp for men to live on the mountain, lumberjacks who felled the trees six days a week, ten hours a day. The logs were taken on horse-driven carts to the saw mill where they were cut into planks. The planks were taken to the railway and shipped to other states, ones that had little to no trees. I had wooed Tom Dunsany into running the company by promising I'd make him rich, and within two years I'd made good on my promise.

The money never stopped coming in. I'd stopped working at the mine site, though I still managed it. This is what took up all my time: checking in on all my businesses, and making sure everything ran smoothly and that my peopled were happy.

I began looking for new places to invest my money. I found that in people, those who'd come to town willing to work hard with an idea and no money to back it. With no collateral, the banks would not even talk to these people. But I know a good worker when I see one, and if they have a dream, all the better. I became that backing. I invested in a dry-goods store, a restaurant, a livery stable, and a few other businesses around town. They all succeeded, not because of me, but because of the people who had a vision and were willing to work hard to make it happen.

In time, I was the richest person in town, including Duncan who'd opened up three other mines that were paying off well.

Being rich is nothing that I or anyone else could imagine. The yearning in your soul never goes away; no matter what you think will end it. Some rich folks think it's more money, so they do whatever it take to make more. Some think it's pleasure, but that never lasts. For me it was only one thing – my children. And for the first time in my life, I was in a position to do something about it.

This is when Paul Morel entered my life. I'd heard about him from a friend of a friend. His office was in New York. He originally worked for the Pinkerton Detective Agency, but went off on his own to start his own agency. He started something new, what became to be known as the "Private Investigator."

I wrote him a letter explaining my wish to find and contact my long-lost children. I received no reply. To emphasize my intentions, I wired him. Still there was no answer. Finally, I wired him again, along with a payment of one thousand dollars. This got his attention. I immediately received a wire from Mr. Morel explaining that he would take up the case, but that it would be very costly, and that the thousand dollars would only be a retainer.

I wired him an additional thousand dollars and a message telling him to take the next train out of New York and come to Denver. A week later, Mr. Morel was knocking at my door.

Paul Morel was a stout little man. His pale, white face was framed by a head of reddish-brown hair with long sideburns that nearly connected to his pointed goatee that was connected to his mustache. He wore a tan suit with a matching vest and a dark brown derby. No doubt, he was made to be a detective. He was not a very notable-looking character, which is probably an asset in his line of work. Handsome folk stand out – you notice them. But folks like Morel are like wallpaper. They go unnoticed and, in turn, get to observe and investigate with ease.

Looking about my humble home, he seemed leery of a black woman who sent two thousand dollars to a stranger, sight unseen, across the country to enlist his services. I didn't feel the need to tell him my story; I felt my money spoke for me. Still, I understood how he would feel hesitant, so I told him anyway.

Again, he warned me of the expense and that there was no guarantee. "I will oversee this case, but mostly my men will be doing the investigation. Understand, I can't guarantee you any results, and you still will pay for our efforts." He told me this as he opened up a contract *for me to sign.* "*You can cancel our services at any time; just know that we will bill you up to the date we receive a wire from you stating so.*"

I signed the contract.

"*You will receive a monthly bill that must be paid immediately, or we will cancel the contract.*"

"*Monthly...?*" *I asked.* "*Do you think it will take that long?*"

"*It's difficult to say,*" *he replied, folding the contract and placing it in his jacket pocket.* "*These things take a lot of time, sometimes years*"

I said nothing, wondering. He grew solemn. "*There is one thing I fear I need to mention. How can I put this without sounding cruel? If we find the location of your family, and they've passed on, you still have to pay the fee. You're paying for our time and effort, not necessarily the results.*"

"*I understand,*" *I told him.*

I walked him to the door. He shook my hand before leaving. "*Have no fear, Mrs. Walker. We will do our very best. I will wire you whenever I have information. You will receive our monthly bill in the post. You have a pleasant day, Mrs. Walker. You are in good hands.*"

With that, he was gone.

I was beside myself with excitement. I truly believed I would someday be reunited with my children. That's when I decided to build the most grand home I or anyone else in Denver could imagine. I spent a fortune on it. I wanted it to look just like the main house of the farm we lived on when we were slaves, before we were sold and separated. I had no idea if my children would even remember. Though it was beyond my powers, I still felt guilty for not being there and not being able to give them the love and guidance a mother should give her children. Somewhere in the back of my mind, I believed if I brought them to a grand home and gave them everything their hearts desired, I could make up for lost time. I believed if I erased all the bad in their lives and sheltered them from any evil happening to them, again, they'd love me. And that's really what it comes down to. I want to love and be loved. But don't we all? If things and money could supply that, it would be a happier world. But we all know it's not so.

I was so hopeful; I didn't even consider at the time that finding my children may not happen, or if it did, that it would be years. I never imagined that Mr. Paul Morel would be a part of my life for the rest of my life.

* * * * * * * *

Months went by without a word from Morel. I kept busy with my life and in time, he rarely crossed my mind. Till one day I received a letter from him. At first, I thought it was just the usual monthly bill from his office. But it was a letter with the most amazing information. I still have the letter. I've kept it all these years, and now it has yellowed with age.

Mrs. Walker,

I hope this letter finds you well. First, let me assure you we have been perusing your requests diligently and your investment is in good hands. I've had a small group of my men investigating records going back years in states and counties you specified. We are mostly looking at government records, auctions and sales, as well as farm and plantation records. We search birth, death, and slave sales records.

The reason for my contacting you is we have come across some old documents of missing, stolen, and runaway slaves in the areas you mentioned. What we have unearthed, I'm sure will come to you as a great surprise, as none of the information you provided me with would suggest this to be true. But we have twice checked our information, and it does seem true.

We have documents that show you had a brother. I know you have no recollection of a brother, as he was much older and escaped from slavery in his teens. I suspect he was never mentioned to you to protect you.

His name was Charles, and went by the name Charles Morris. His flight took him to Florida where he fled to the deep marsh country. He lived there alone, rarely seen, and became quite a legend among the locals. He never bothered them, and they never bothered him.

But there is a strange and sad twist to the story of Charles Morris. He became acquainted with and eventually had a love affair with one of the local white women, a young widow named Patricia Guairá. The affair didn't last long; your brother Charles was hung by local vigilantes for his crime: his affair with a white woman.

The affair resulted in Miss Guairá having Charles' baby, a male child. For her involvement with a black man, she was shunned by family, friends, and the white community. She has lived in the black community of the county these past years, raising your nephew as best she can.

As if this story weren't sad enough, there is more. As of our last inquiry, Patricia Guairá, your so-called sister-in-law, is dying and may possibly be dead by the time you read this.

We can pursue this further, if that is your wish. Enclosed in this envelope are the documents stating all I have told you, and the location of Miss Patricia Guairá and your nephew.

I wait patiently for your reply.

Yours truly,

Paul Morel

I wrote Morel to do nothing about what he'd learned about my brother and his family. I spoke with Duncan and all the folks managing my affairs, and told them of my intentions. I was off to Florida.

Chapter XVIII

This Side of Heaven

They say that God doesn't place anything in a person's life they can't handle. It would seem He has a high opinion of us. There are many things in a person's life that can only be described as unbearable.

For Etta Jean, it was the day Mrs. Ford asked for a doctor's help.

"But Faye's been doing so well," Etta Jean commented.

"She was," Mrs. Ford replied. "But lately she's been looking poorly. Her lungs sound full of liquid. We need to send for a doctor."

So Etta Jean called for a doctor. Again, having money made things possible. The best doctor in town was, Doctor Sanford, an ancient, little white man with one white hair on his head for each of the many years he'd served the county. Everyone trusted Doctor Sanford, but few could afford him.

After examining Faye for what seemed too short a time, Doctor Sanford stood in the hallway speaking softly to Etta Jean and Mrs. Ford. "I'm afraid it's pneumonia."

Both women fell silent, knowing how serious it was. With her medical background and knowledge, Mrs. Ford looked about to cry. In her years, she'd seen so many die of this disease.

"What can we do?" Etta Jean finally asked.

"Keep her in bed and let her rest. Make sure she drinks plenty of water. I'll give her a prescription that will keep her comfortable. We can only wait and pray."

When the doctor left, Etta Jean looked to Mrs. Ford for comfort but found none, only a look of hopelessness.

"What's wrong?" Etta Jean asked.

"It's her age. I've never seen an older person who has it this bad survive. They usually last no more than a few weeks, and then suffer the entire time," Mrs. Ford replied sorrowfully.

"She'll be fine," Etta Jean said. But it was only wishful thinking, and she knew it.

****

"What's wrong with Auntie Faye?" Liberty asked as she sat on her mother's lap.

"She's very sick. It's her lungs; they're filled with water."

"Why don't you turn her upside down and let the water out?" the naïve little girl asked, truly concerned and serious.

"If that would work, we would. But it's sticky water and doesn't come out that easy."

"Why can't I see Auntie Faye?"

"Because the sickness is catching, especially to little girls, and Auntie Faye doesn't want you to be sick."

"Is Auntie Faye going to die?"

It was a difficult question to answer to a small child. You want to always tell the truth, but you also want to protect them. Etta Jean decided to play it safe and sit on the fence.

"We hope she don't, sweetheart. You just keep praying that Auntie Faye gets better."

* * * * * * * *

Etta Jean and Mrs. Ford took turns watching over Faye. Etta Jean did not allow anyone else, in fear of Faye being contagious. But it was too much for even two people. Finally, she hired a nurse that Doctor Sanford recommended.

Nurse Bernice Wesley was a cold fish. Her bedside manners were minimal. She was an elderly white woman with a cold stare. She showed little concern for anyone, let alone her patient. She was not one to discriminate. Black or white, she treated equally with disrespect. But she knew her job and she did it well. If the patient needed moving, or cleaning, or a drink of water, she did a thorough job of it and without ever complaining. She was a professional nurse. She was the best, and she knew it.

They scheduled Nurse Wesley to watch over from midnight till six o'clock in the morning. Etta Jean and Mrs. Ford took turns relieving Nurse Wesley.

One morning, Etta Jean entered Faye's bedroom. Nurse Wesley sat at her bedside. Being the professional she was, she was wide-awake, sitting quietly and watching over her patient, not even reading. The sunlight was just beginning to enter the room through the windows.

"How did she do last night?" Etta Jean asked.

"Not well," replied Nurse Wesley as she gathered her belongings to leave. "Her lungs are filling."

"Should we call the doctor?"

"She doesn't need a doctor; she needs a priest," Nurse Wesley said coldly. Etta Jean was shocked by the woman's honesty, but she knew she was right. "I doubt if she lasts the week," Nurse Wesley added as she made for the bedroom door.

There was a guttural moan from Faye. Obviously, the woman was awake and heard the conversation.

"I wish you'd be more discreet when you speak in front of Faye. She's not unaware and she's not stupid," Etta Jean scolded.

"Sorry, but you asked and I told you. Next time, don't ask. I'll see you tonight," Nurse Wesley said as she left the room.

Etta Jean looked at Faye's face. There was a sad and worried look there.

Perhaps, Nurse Wesley put the notion in her head because Etta Jean did not know why she said what she did.

"Would you like to see a preacher?" Etta Jean asked.

Faye grunted and blinked her eyes once, which meant "Yes,"

That afternoon, Etta Jean sent Miriam to fetch the Reverend Dewitt Addison to visit with Faye. The minister at the still-only black church in town was more than happy to oblige. After a day of pastoral duties, he arrived at eight o'clock in the evening.

Etta Jean was the first to greet him. "Thank you, Reverend, for coming. Have you eaten? I can have the kitchen make you something."

"No, thank you. I'm sure my wife is keeping something warm for me. I'd hate to disappoint her by coming home with a full stomach. Now, tell me the situation and about your friend."

They whispered as they climbed the stairs. Etta Jean told Reverend Addison everything she knew about Faye.

"She sounds like a good woman," the reverend said.

"She is, Reverend."

"Then let's put her soul in the Lord's hands," he said, opening the door to Faye's bedroom. "I can take it from here," he told Etta Jean, leaving her staring at the closed door.

It was a long wait. Etta Jean wondered what the Reverend could be saying to Faye. After all, it could only be a one-sided conversation. It was nearly ten when Reverend Addison came out of the bedroom. He was smiling.

"I know my wife," he said. "She'll be mad as a wet hen when I get home. She'll never understand it's just part of the job."

"What happened?" Etta Jean asked.

"The best of what could happen, happened," he said. "I'm not a smart man. There is much in this world I do not understand. But I do know I am destined for the Promised Land and so is Sister Faye."

Etta Jean showed the reverend to the front door.

"So, will Sister Faye and I see you on the other side?"

Etta Jean didn't have an answer.

Reverend Addison just smiled.

"When you're ready, you know where to find me," he said as he walked from the house into the darkness.

* * * * * * * *

It was on a night Nurse Wesley couldn't stay the entire night. Mrs. Ford took watch over Faye at three in the morning. Etta Jean lay in her bed, unable to sleep. Too much ran through her mind. She got out of bed and looked in on Liberty. The child slept motionless and peaceful.

She decided to look in on Faye and Mrs. Ford. She thought of knocking on Faye's bedroom door but, for some reason, didn't. She opened the door slowly and quietly.

Entering the dark room, there was just enough light to make out shapes. Why Mrs. Ford didn't have a lamp burning was a mystery to Etta Jean. Standing in the bedroom doorway, Etta Jean saw Mrs. Ford standing over Faye. As she walked forward, she saw that Mrs. Ford held a pillow over Faye's face. She was suffocating her.

Without a second thought or concern for her own safety, Etta Jean rushed forward and pushed Mrs. Ford away from the bedside. The pillow fell off Faye's face. The sound of the woman taking in needed air filled the room. Etta Jean hit Mrs. Ford so hard the old woman fell to the floor. She lay motionless for a time.

"Are you all right?" Etta Jean asked.

"I'll be fine," Mrs. Ford said, catching her breath.

Etta Jean reached down and helped Mrs. Ford to her feet. The woman scurried to the chair at bedside and fell into it.

"What were you doing?" Etta Jean demanded.

"She should have died weeks ago," Mrs. Ford said. "She keeps hanging on in misery. I couldn't stand to watch her suffer anymore."

"And what if she can recover?" Etta Jean asked.

"She's not going to recover, and you know it. She's bound to die soon."

"And the time of her death will be between her and God. It's not your decision," Etta Jean said. "I want you out of here within the hour. I'll give you a month's salary, but I want you gone before sunup."

"But where will I go?" Mrs. Ford pleaded. "I was only trying to help."

"I understand," Etta Jean said. "But your kind of help isn't wanted here. I want you gone."

Mrs. Ford didn't argue. She left Faye's room, went to her own room, and packed.

An hour later, Etta Jean met Mrs. Ford at the front door. She handed her a wad of cash – two months wages, more than she said she would give her.

The two women looked sadly into each other's eyes. They loved each other and would miss each other, but Etta Jean could not have such things go on in her home. It was not something she taught to Liberty, and certainly not the way she lived.

Mrs. Ford knew there was nothing to say. Without a word, she took her pay and left. Etta Jean slowly and softly closed the front door.

* * * * * * *

The next few weeks were difficult. Faye was still holding on, always in pain. There were times Etta Jean thought that perhaps Mrs. Ford had the right idea. Maybe it was a more merciful way. Was she only allowing Faye to live for her benefit and not Faye's? But somehow she couldn't see things that way.

It was in the dead of night, during Nurse Wesley's watch that Etta Jean woke from a tapping on her door. In the dark, she got out of bed and opened the door. It was Nurse Wesley.

"I think you should go to her. I don't think she'll make it to the morning," Nurse Wesley whispered.

"Are you sure?" Etta Jean asked, rubbing the sleep from her eyes.

"I've been doing this kind of work since before you were born. I ought to know death when I see it," Nurse Wesley said in her usual cold manner. "I've seen it hundreds of times. Your friend won't make the dawn."

Etta Jean put on her housecoat and followed Nurse Wesley to Faye's bedroom. Etta Jean sat on the edge of Faye's bed and gently brushed the hair from the dying woman's forehead.

"Can we have some time alone?" Etta Jean asked Nurse Wesley who without a word turned and left the room.

Etta Jean continued to stroke Faye's forehead. The room was dark with just enough moonlight coming in from the windows to flood it a deep ocean blue.

Faye moaned slightly.

"Don't worry, Faye. I'm here and I won't leave you," Etta Jean whispered.

The Bible is full of miracles. If you have faith, you believe them to be real. If not, you think of them as pleasant myths or instructive stories. But for those who have witnessed a miracle firsthand, their lives are never the same. This was what happened between Etta Jean and Faye. It is well-known by people who work with the dying that even a person in a coma can wake for their dying moment to say goodbye.

"I know you are there, and I thank you for all you've done for me," Faye said softly. Etta Jean was taken aback into silence.

"Don't worry about me, Etta Jean. I'm not afraid anymore, Reverend Addison seen to that. It's all part of life. I thank you for all your sweetness. Give my love to Liberty. Give my love to everyone. Tell them there's nothing to fear. God bless everyone."

With that, she took in a long, deep breath. Etta Jean held Faye's hand. It tightened around hers. Then Faye let out her last breath, slow and long. With each moment, Etta Jean realized Faye's breath and her grip on Etta Jean's hand lessened. Till finally, the breath was gone and the grip was no longer.

There was a peace in the room, a peace Etta Jean had never experienced or expected. It may sound mad, but she could feel Faye's spirit leave her body and then hover over the room for a moment. Then the next moment, her spirit was swept away like a gentle wind. Etta Jean could feel the spirit was gone and that she was alone. She thought at the moment of Faye's death she would feel sad and remorseful. But instead, she sat on the edge of the bed, still holding Faye's hand, experiencing the most joy she ever knew possible. It was as close to bliss as one on this side of heaven can experience.

Chapter XIX

A Sister's Promise

Technically, the war was over, but not much had changed. The South was still the South, and even over six hundred thousand deaths weren't going to change that – not anytime soon.

In the old days, a black woman, if she was a slave, usually traveled safely, it was considered bad manners tampering with another man's property, as you most certainly didn't want them tampering with your property. Of course, there were men who didn't pay heed to the unwritten law, but they were usually strangers to the area, or locals who would soon regret their foolishness.

Now with the war over, and no one allowed to own another – this was on paper only – a traveling black woman moved about in danger. No longer protected by the unwritten code, anyone, black or white, felt free to do whatever they wished. And no one would stop them, including the authorities.

But a free black woman, one of great wealth, from the North traveling through the South, was taking her life in her hands. There would be few friends, if any, on this journey, which is why I purchased a gun in Denver.

It would take many trains and even more days to get down to Florida. I could only hope I was not too late.

When I crossed over the Mason-Dixon Line into the South, you could feel and see the difference. The war had left the South in disarray. Towns were left demolished. On farms and plantations, the soil was now bloodred with nothing growing in it. It was clear what damage was done, and it would take years to recover.

At each layover, I stayed at a black hotel in a black neighborhood, but still I did not feel safe. I dared not go out at night, even to a restaurant. Everywhere, lawlessness abounded, and if there were laws, there was no one to enforce them. When I wasn't on a train, my hand was in my purse, on my gun. In the hotels, I slept with my gun under my pillow.

I didn't need to look out the window of the train to know we were traveling south. The heat in the car grew with each hour, till it was like being in an oven.

Sadly, the last train took me to Tallahassee in the northern part of Florida, just south of the Georgia state line. I needed to go farther south. There were coaches that traveled to the area I needed to go. I was confronted with resistance and forced to pay twice the price of the other passengers – white passengers. But what could I do? Who could I complain to? I could only think myself blessed to be able to afford the price.

Thankfully, the carriage passed through Cross City, my destination. It was a small and sparsely populated city not far from the Gulf and on the southern edge of the wetlands. It was the county seat, of all places, in Dixie County.

There was a melancholy air about the place. It was never very prosperous, what with the sea to the west and the wetlands to the north. It was not good farmland. But now with the end of the Civil War, it was pitiful, and the population had fallen to half of what it once was.

Small town or not, it was easy to see which part of town was where the blacks lived and where the whites lived. In the black part of town, I headed for the steeple that was visible from afar. I was greeted by the Reverend Tim Cooley and his wife, Desiree. They took me in immediately and offered me a cup of tea.

"Poor Miss Patricia Guairá and her young son. She was from a wealthy Portuguese family. They abandoned her as soon as they knew she was involved with a black man, as did all the other white folk in the area."

"And many of the black folk as well," Mrs. Cooley added.

"Sad to say, that is true," Reverend Cooley agreed. "An interracial affair is something both sides despise. Many so-called Christians turned their backs on her because they never married. There's been much unchristian behavior in this city, I'm afraid to say."

"I need to see her. Charlie was my brother," I said.

"Finish your tea, and I'll take you to her," Reverend Cooley said.

"You must stay with us," Mrs. Cooley added.

"I thank you for that," I said.

* * * * * * *

The home of Patricia Guairá was less than a shack. It was a one-room box with nothing more than a table and a bed. An old black woman sat in a bedside chair, quietly and patiently keeping watch. On that bed laid the dying Patricia Guairá. It was pneumonia, and she was hopelessly in its last stages.

Her eyes were closed. She was as thin as a stick and as white as the sheets that covered her.

"Patricia, there's someone here to see you," Reverend Cooley whispered.

She tried to open her eyes, but was only able to open one. She smiled when she saw Reverend Cooley.

"This is Elizabeth Walker. She's come a long way to see you."

She turned her head slightly to look at me. She smiled, I smiled back.

"I don't know how to say this. I'm Charles' sister," I told her.

Her eyes went wide. Suddenly, she was more alert. She almost seemed as if she would sit up.

"Charlie never said he had a sister," she moaned out the words.

"He was much older. He left home before I was born," I explained.

"I loved him so much," she said, breaking into tears

Reverend Cooley pulled me to the side and whispered to me. "Charlie lived alone in the wetlands. He became something of a legend in these parts. How these two got together, I'll never know. They kept their affair a secret for years. But when Patricia became with child, there was no way to hide it. An angry mob found Charlie and hanged him. They let him hang for three days, and then they cut him down and tossed his body into the wetlands for the alligators. He didn't even have a decent funeral. The church folks have been helping her and her boy since then. Now that she's like this, I don't know what's to happen to him."

I returned to her bedside, reached down, and took hold of her hand. She looked up at me, her face wet with tears.

"You're my Charles' sister…you're family. I'll be gone soon. My boy won't have a home or a family. You gotta take him for your own, my sister."

I didn't have to think twice. I knew what I needed to do.

"Don't you worry none. I'll take him for my own," I promised.

She turned her head on her pillow and looked at the old woman who'd been caring for her. "Call him for, me, please?" she asked the woman.

The old woman hobbled over to the front door and hollered, "Jaggers…Jaggers… your momma wants you!"

* * * * * * * *

Jaggers was around nine or ten when we first met. He was tall for his age and very slender. His cherub face was solemn with a faraway look in his eye, like a child who had experienced and seen more than any child should. His skin and features were that of his mother's – pale white with sandy brown hair and grayish blue eyes. He was a smart child. He knew what was going on around him. He understood and suffered in deep silence.

Naming him Jaggers came about in an unusual manner. During their private and secret life together, Patricia taught Charlie how to read, another sin according to Southern slave owners. One of his favorite books was Great Expectations by Charles Dickens. One of the characters was named Jaggers. Not wanting to burden his son with the name of a well-known slave for the rest of his life, Charlie gave his son one name – Jaggers. Patricia understood and agreed.

Strangely enough, the Jaggers in the book was a lawyer, and in time, the young Jaggers felt the calling to study law. He grew up to become a talented lawyer.

We stayed close to Patricia's side, day and night, for the next week. Her strength waned, her eyes clouded, and her breathing faltered. With each passing day, there was less of what she was, till one day there was none of her.

She spent her last hours with a small group of women from the church praying and singing hymns over her. Unable to speak, she held on tightly to her son's hand.

Finally, as a new day began, she breathed her last. Her hand fell from Jaggers'. The child didn't cry. His pain was so deep; it would take time to reach the surface.

There was no funeral. They put the body in a makeshift coffin and marched her down to the cemetery – the black cemetery, among the only people who'd accepted her.

There were a few folks from the church, singing hymns as they lowered the body. I can still remember Reverend Cooley's words: "Lord, we commend to you the soul of our sister. And she is truly our sister. And for those of us who know it, we give thanks. And for those who do not, we raise them up in prayer."

There was a small luncheon afterwards at the church. I sat young Jaggers down and tried to explain our situation. He could live with me in Denver, if he wanted. He said not a word, and just nodded his approval.

Two days later, we caught the coach to Tallahassee, where we'd catch the series of trains to take us to Colorado. It was interesting, traveling with a little white boy. Where I once traveled in fear as a black woman, much of the danger was gone. Folks looked at us and thought this must be some well-off white boy traveling with his mammy. No one seemed interested in disturbing our travels. For this reason, we were allowed to travel first-class, whereas before, alone, I could not. We still stayed at black hotels. Most folks didn't think twice about this, knowing I would not be given accommodations in a white hotel. As well, no black man would so much as look at us sideways, in fear of white citizens who watched over their own. There would be hell to pay if either one of us were molested or cheated.

The journey was hard for Jaggers. He'd buried his mother, and each mile took him farther away from her memory, toward a new life he had no idea as to what it would be like. He spoke little and ate seldom, usually only a few bites. Often at night, he'd wake from a deep sleep, screaming or crying or both. I tried to comfort him, but he seemed to want his space to morn and be left alone.

It was somewhere midway in our journey. We were traveling by train in a first-class apartment. We were alone. I was looking out the window, watching the sunset. The plains of the flatlands reflected the purple and orange that lit up the sky. Jaggers sat at my side, watching with me.

Suddenly, most unexpectedly, he slipped his hand into mine, rested his head on my shoulder, and fell fast asleep. It was just the beginning of our life together, but I smiled, knowing we'd taken the first step.

Chapter XX

Don't Be Afraid

After reading her mother's journal concerning Jaggers, Etta Jean was in a strange state of mind. She was confused, angry, and glad, all at once. She was determined to corner Jaggers and discuss the matter, but not until after Faye's funeral.

Determined to give Faye a grand sendoff, Etta Jean had contacted Reverend Dewitt and told him money was no problem. The church was decorated with an array of flowers. The piano was tuned. And the choir came in full force, dressed in long, flowing, red robes.

The church was filled with people Etta Jean didn't know, mostly business acquaintances of her mother who'd come to pay their respects. The ceremony went off as planned. The choir sang like angels, and Reverend Dewitt gave a eulogy that any dignitary would be proud of.

Unexpectedly, though customary, Reverend Dewitt asked if there was anyone who'd like to come up and say a few words about Faye. Etta Jean did not want to stand up in front of strangers and speak, but she felt compelled to do so. If she didn't, then there would be no words spoken – and Faye deserved more than words.

Etta Jean raised her hand as she rose and walked to the front of the church. Reverend Dewitt stepped aside. All eyes were on Etta Jean.

"Most of you never knew Faye Wilkins, which is a shame; she was a great woman. Most of you knew my mother; this, too, is a shame because I never knew my mother. I hear she was a great woman, also.

"But I wasn't a motherless child. For all purposes, Faye Wilkins was my mother. If you want to know what she was like, just think of a loving mother.

"That's all I have to say. She was loved by all who knew her, and she will be missed."

Etta Jean went back to her seat. Her words moved everyone, but those who knew Faye were in tears. Reverend Dewitt closed with a prayer. Six strong men lifted the coffin and slowly carried it out of the church and into the hearse.

There were buggies to take close friends to the small graveyard a quarter mile behind the great house Etta Jean's mother built.

There were only three people in the buggy directly behind the hearse; in it were Etta Jean, Liberty, and Jaggers.

Everyone was solemn. Liberty was beside herself with grief; her eyes were swollen from crying. Etta Jean held her close.

"We need to talk," Etta Jean directed her gaze and words to Jaggers. "When we get back to the house, we need to talk."

An impish grin appeared on Jaggers' face. "It would seem you've come to the part in your mother's diary concerning yours truly," he said. Etta Jean did not reply.

Just as the procession passed the main house on its way to the family cemetery, Jaggers made a statement that send chills down Etta Jean's spine.

"In all your time living here at the main house, you've never visited your mother's grave. You're finally going to get to see it."

Etta Jean knew what she felt was foolish and childish, but she couldn't help it.

"Stop right here, driver," Etta Jean said, tapping the buggy driver's shoulder. "Stop right here; I want to get out."

When the buggy halted, Etta Jean took Liberty's hand and got out.

"What are you doing?" Jaggers asked.

"I can't do this; I just can't do this."

"Do what?"

"I don't want to see my mother's grave, at least not now."

"I don't understand," Jaggers questioned.

"But, Momma, I want to say goodbye to Auntie Faye," Liberty pleaded.

"You've already said your goodbyes. Come, we're going home."

The child fell into a fit of crying and pulling against her mother's grip.

"I'll take her," Jaggers said. "Don't do this to the child."

Etta Jean knew he was right. She did her best to calm Liberty and helped her back into the buggy. Liberty fell into Jaggers' arms, crying against his suit lapel.

"I'm sorry. I just can't right now," Etta Jean said as the buggy pulled away, and she headed for the house.

****

Later in the library, Etta Jean and Jaggers sat over tea.

"I'm sorry for the way I acted," Etta Jean said to Jaggers.

"There's no need to apologize." Jaggers smiled kindly. "You've been through much, and I can understand that you're trying to make sense of it all."

"And I want to thank you for taking Liberty to the gravesite."

"My pleasure. She's a great child." He leaned closer and spoke softly. "If there's anyone you need to apologize to, it's your little girl. You scared her."

"I know, and I will. I feel so embarrassed."

"Like I said, there's no need for that," he replied.

There was a long moment of silence. When it became too uncomfortable, Etta Jean spoke.

"So now what?" she asked.

"What do you mean?"

"I mean, do I call you cousin, brother, or what?"

"Well, you can just call me Jaggers."

"And you can just call me Etta Jean."

The two smiled and then began to laugh at the absurdity of it all.

"But I don't understand," Etta Jean questioned, "why didn't you just come right out and tell me who you were?"

"It was all part of Momma's plan. She felt you needed to learn everything, but slowly so you could understand it better. It seems things aren't working out the way she planned it."

"It sounds so strange to hear you call her Momma."

"Why? Is it because I'm white?"

"No...no...that's not the reason. It's because she had children, and none of us got to be with her or know her, but you did. I guess you can say I'm jealous."

"I can understand that."

"But that's what brings me to wonder about you. If she raised you as her own, why am I getting all the rewards? Why did she leave me everything?"

Jaggers smiled. "Let me explain. Firstly, I'm far from destitute; Momma left me a very wealthy man. And I do have a lucrative law practice, thanks to her sending me to some of the best schools in the country.

"You need to understand, your mother wanted so badly to give to you so much. It's not the money, the business, or the property and house; she wanted to give of herself. And that's what she was, a great businesswoman. She wanted to give you her life. You don't have to accept it, just know that it's yours, and she gave it to you. If you will only follow the path she's left for you, you may understand her better, and you may find happiness as well."

They both stopped speaking and continued drinking their tea. When he'd finished, Jaggers rose.

"Please excuse me; I need to get back to my office."

"Where do you live?" asked Etta Jean.

"I have a large home on the other end of town. Not as large as this one, but I don't need as much. Perhaps sometime you can come over with Liberty for dinner."

"That would be nice."

When he got to the door, Etta Jean called out, "Jaggers? I'm glad we had this talk. If you don't mind, now and then, might I call you brother?"

"Only if now and then I can call you sister," he said as he opened the door. He turned to look at her before leaving. "Oh, and one day we'll visit Momma's grave. I think it will bring you some peace."

****

There was an uncomfortable air between Etta Jean and Liberty that day. Etta Jean felt embarrassed by the way she acted on the way to the cemetery. Liberty had never seen her mother in such a state, and it scared her. For the rest of the day, they spoke little and avoided eye contact. Etta Jean knew she had caused the rift between them, and that she would need to be the one to cross it. But with others around, it was impossible to speak of something so personal. Etta Jean waited till Liberty's bedtime.

Sitting on the edge of Liberty's bed, Etta Jean did her best to explain her actions.

"I want to apologize for the way I acted today. I know I scared you, and that's something I never wanted to do. Will you please forgive me?"

"I never knew mothers could ask for forgiveness," Liberty said shyly.

"Mothers make mistakes, too, just like everyone else."

Liberty thought this through and smiled. It seemed to comfort her; but it confused her as well. Children never think of their parents as ordinary people. And when they do learn this fact, they are usually much older. It saddened Etta Jean that Liberty learned it so young.

"Why didn't you want to say goodbye to Auntie Faye?"

"Oh, honey, I did. I wanted so much to be there. I loved Auntie Faye. But I was afraid to go."

"Afraid?" Liberty asked, bewildered again to hear that her mother could be afraid of anything – another fact about their parents children don't learn till they are much older. Parents are supposed to be brave and fearless.

"What were you afraid of?"

"My mother, your grandmother, is buried in that cemetery, too. I never knew my mother, and I'm just beginning to learn who she was. Even in the grave, I'm just not ready to meet her. I'm afraid..."

"Don't be afraid, Momma. Mothers are the nicest people in the world."

Etta Jean sighed with relief that her daughter had at least one fallacy left to believe in. Etta Jean swore she would do anything in the world for her daughter to keep believing that way.

Liberty sat up in bed and wrapped her arms around her mother's neck.

"Oh, Momma, I love you."

That was all Etta Jean needed to hear to make everything right again.

"I love you, too, baby."

Chapter XXI

I Love You for It

I knew the road ahead for Jaggers and me would be a rough one. I just didn't have a clue of what obstacles there would be. The best we could do was face them when confronted with them, and do our best.

The first problem was Jaggers. He was in a new home, with new people and a new life, and his mother had just died. It took so much time, understanding, and patience. I could afford his heart's desires, but spoiling him to soothe him would only deter him from being the man that I and, I'm sure, his mother would want him to be. But how do you steer a child from the sorrow of death?

It took a long time, but eventually Jaggers settled in, and our relationship grew closer and more comfortable. Still, there was a tension that needed to be addressed. It took much soul-searching of my pride, but in time I realized the unseen problem was me.

Firstly, though I loved Jaggers dearly, I felt annoyed. Somewhere out there were my children. I not only missed them so, I was rich and wanted to make their lives better. Not knowing where they were was torture. They deserved to be pampered, but it was not to be. Yet, here was their cousin reaping all the benefits of his rich aunt. I would never deny anything to Jaggers. But it felt off-center, and it played with my emotions.

Secondly, I was jealous of Jaggers. We were from the same family, of the same blood, but all the obstacles that plagued my life daily didn't even exist for him. Wherever I went with him, I was looked down as his servant. They would look at his white skin and my black skin and assume I worked for his parents. They never would think I was his parent. It was often the same when I was with Christina. They would look at this pretty white girl, and I was the colored girl. I fought it tooth and nail all my life, but sometimes you get tired. And it was all the worse with Jaggers, because I was the parent, yet often I was treated like the colored girl.

It was difficult to overcome, but I knew I had to for Jaggers' sake, and for my own. Going through life with a chip on your shoulder will tilt you in the wrong direction every time.

Once Jaggers settled in, I knew I needed to enroll him in school. But when I tested him on different subjects, I realized he'd not been taught well. He would be so far behind the other children of his age. So before enrolling him in school, I hired a tutor to bring him up to snuff.

Her name was Eleanor Honing. Miss Honing was new to the area and came with many references praising her teaching abilities. She was a hatchet-faced woman, her features reminiscent of a scarecrow. I would guess she was in her thirties, but it was hard to tell. She had the type of face that made her look ancient. I would imagine she looked like an old woman even when she was a little girl, if she ever was a little girl. She was always serious and never smiled. When she came to the house, she spoke to me in a very condescending manner. Strangely, I didn't take offence to this. I realized she took up this tone of superiority with everyone. It wasn't because Miss Honing was prejudiced; there was room for everyone at the end of her nose to be looked down upon.

I was in a hurry to get Jaggers into a school, to get him in a normal child's routine, so I hired Miss Honing to visit Monday through Friday for two hours in the afternoon. She was like clockwork, arriving at three and not leaving till the clocks struck five.

Jaggers did not like Miss Honing. She made him very uncomfortable. But it was clear Jaggers was improving, so I continued with Miss Honing's services, much to Jaggers' chagrin. His only comfort was in knowing it would only be for a few weeks.

One night during supper, I noticed Jaggers acting strange. He was quiet, picking at his food, and lost in thought.

"Jaggers, are you all right?"

"I guess so," he replied matter-a-factly.

"You guess so? I've never seen you eat less than four pieces of fried chicken, and you haven't even touched your first piece. Now, tell me what's wrong."

He sighed heavily. "It's Miss Honing…"

"Oh, her again. Don't worry; it'll only be a few more weeks."

"It's not that," he said, holding out his hand that he kept hidden under the table. The hand was brushed with bloody red lines across from his wrist to his knuckles.

"Did she do that to you?" I asked

He nodded.

"Why did she do that to you?" I asked him.

"I couldn't get the sums right. I tried, I really tried," was his answer.

The next day when Miss Honing arrived, I summoned her to my office. I offered her a seat. My first thought was to give her a piece of my mind, or worse, but I made a silent vow to remain calm.

I handed her an envelope. Surprised, she took it and looked inside.

"That is the remainder of the money we agreed upon for your services plus a small bonus for any inconvenience. We will no longer need your services," I told her coldly.

"*And may I know why I'm being dismissed?*" she asked.

I looked her square in the eye. "*Because we don't beat children here, Miss Honing. Now, if you could please leave.*"

"*I only hit him for his own good; he's a slow learner,*" she insisted.

"*And hitting him till you drew blood would make him learn faster?*" I asked sarcastically.

"*This is ridiculous!*" she shouted. "*I want to talk to your superior.*"

I felt the anger building inside. "*In this house, I don't have a superior,*" I flung my words at her.

"*Well, his parents – how can I speak with Jaggers' parents? I insist on speaking with his parents. I'm tired of having to do business with the house's top colored girl,*" she spurted out at me.

I jumped from my seat and pointed to the door. "*I am his parent, and I say I want you out of here!*" I was shouting at this point.

She was clearly disturbed and angry, but refusing to argue. She marched to the door. "*You should all go back to where you came from,*" she said as she stormed out the door.

I thought of a million things I wanted to scream back at her. Then I realized I would only be stooping to her level. I understood then and there that there is no cure for stupidity.

****

I enrolled Jaggers at the finest school in the city. Actually, to be honest, I had Christina enroll him. It was a very posh white school. I knew they would accept him, his skin being so fair. But I was afraid if I were involved it would hurt his chances of being accepted. Don't misunderstand, it took a lot for me to back down and do it that way. I'm a proud black woman; I never back down. But my love for Jaggers was too great, and I wasn't going to let my pride stand in the way of his future.

I remember how Christina pleaded with me not to be the one to enroll him.

"*They won't believe he's my son,*" she said. "*I'm not old enough.*"

"*Of course you are,*" I argued. "*You just had him when you were young.*"

"*But I'm not married,*" she said.

"*That don't stop people from having babies,*" I said.

"*Can't I at least tell them my husband died in the war?*" she finally begged me.

"*Go ahead, if it makes you feel more respectable,*" I laughed. "*But don't tell them what side he fought on. There are folks from both sides around here, and one side may not cotton to another.*"

She seemed to like that answer. So that's how we got Jaggers into the finest white school in the city – heck, in the entire state of Colorado.

Well, for the longest time, things went just fine. As for Jaggers, he was doing well in school. He was making friends, and he was very popular.

Christina would drop him off at school in the morning and pick him up in the afternoon. Jaggers and I became very close. We spent hours of quality time together, and we went to the black church on Sundays. But in public life, I'd stand in the background, if not completely invisible. Oh, I believed at the time it was the best thing I could do for Jaggers. But looking back now, I know I was wrong.

I was helping and promoting him in the white world, where I knew he would fit in with no problem. But I was robbing him of his birthright. Yes, he had a white mother, but he had two parents like everyone else in this world, and his father was black.

Black blood ran in his veins as well as white. He was as much a black person as he was a white person. And I was denying that part of him to grow and flourish. It was I who was hiding these facts like it was something to be ashamed of. Well, I was wrong; and I learned how wrong it was in the most brutal, amazing, surprising, and challenging way.

One late afternoon, Christina met Jaggers at the school to bring him home. I saw them approaching the house. When I opened the door to greet him, he rushed past me and ran up to his room.

I asked Christina what was the matter.

She shook her head. "I don't know; he was upset when we left the school. I asked him what was wrong, but he wouldn't tell me," she said.

I went upstairs to Jaggers' room and knocked on the door. Of course, he told me to go away. But I told him that wasn't going to be, and he needed to open up.

When he opened the door, I could see he'd been crying.

"I need to come in," I told him.

He stepped aside; I entered and sat on the edge of his bed.

"So tell me, what's wrong?" I asked.

He took a moment to think. The story went like this. It seems the school had a new teacher, and of all people it was Miss Honing. The bitter woman took no time before informing everyone who his mother was. Needless to say, Jaggers had a rough day.

"They called me names. All my friends turned on me," Jaggers told me in tears. He fell to his knees and placed his head in my lap. "Oh, Momma, don't make me go back there, please, Momma, please," he cried.

This was the first time Jaggers ever called me "Momma." I had always hoped someday he would. It was bittersweet for it to happen under those circumstances.

"Baby, I'm sorry this happened to you," I said. "Sometimes life can be cruel. But you've got to be strong and learn something from it." I held his hand and looked at it. "You got white blood and black blood running through your veins. You can't go through life sitting on the fence, jump this way when it's best and that way when the wind's blowing that way. You got to be who you are. And some people are going to hate you for that, but other folks will love you for it. I love you for it. You got to go back to that school and stand up to them or you'll be on your knees for the rest of your life."

"But they don't let blacks in our school," he wept.

"Don't worry. Just let Momma take care of it. It will all work out. Now, clean yourself up and come downstairs for supper. I love you," I said as I kissed his forehead.

He didn't say a word; he just hugged me like I was the only safe place in the world.

* * * * * * * *

I didn't sleep well that night. I had to make a decision as to how I would handle Jaggers' school situation. My first reaction was to lash out. Go down to the school in the morning and give them what for. But that was just an emotional response. You don't change the course of a river by throwing stones into it.

The next morning, I accompanied Jaggers to school. I could tell he was nervous, but he kept his head up and acted like it was any other day. I was so proud of him.

When I saw him to the school's front door, I entered with him. He went to class and I headed for the principal's office. I knocked on the door and waited for a response.

"Come in." It was a deep growl of a voice.

Principal Tallmadge Russell was the spitting image of Moses in a modern day suit. The only thing he lacked was a staff in his hand. He was wrinkled with age, his hair gray and long. A salt and pepper beard covered his chest nearly down to his waist, and a mustache hid his upper lip. Still seated behind his desk, he positioned his glasses on the edge of his nose to see over the frames to look at me.

"Yes, may I help you?" he asked, sounding perturbed.

"My name is Elizabeth Walker; I'm Jaggers' mother," I told him.

"Yes, I've heard of you. Miss Honing told me about you and your boy. You're not really the boy's mother, are you?"

"I'm his aunt. But I am his sole guardian," I said.

"Well, if that's the case," he said cold as ice. "We don't allow coloreds in this school. So, I'm afraid you'll just have to leave and take your boy with you," he said with a tone of final dismissal.

"First off, we're not colored," I said, sitting down in the chair in front of his desk.

"What do you think you're doing?" he snarled at me.

"You said you know who I am; do you really?" I asked.

"Yes, I do. I asked around about you. I understand you're a very wealthy woman. I don't hold it against anyone, white or negro," he emphasized that word "negro," knowing the term "colored" didn't sit well with me, and not wanting any trouble. "But rules are rules. We don't accept…Negros here. So, I wish you a good day," he said in conclusion.

I reached over and took a slip of paper and a pen from off his desk.

"What do you think you're doing?" he said, sounding very angry.

I wrote a very large amount on the slip of paper and placed it and the pen back down on the desk, facing him.

"That is the amount of money I'm willing to donate to the school if you change your admittance policy," I said, smiling at him.

His eyes went wide, and the slip of paper wavered in his shaking hand.

"Why, this is more than we paid for this entire building," he exclaimed, his tone changing dramatically and quickly. "I suppose we can make some changes to accommodate your needs," he said. He was all smiles now.

He stood up and offered his hand to me. In the back of my mind, I wanted to spit in his eye, but knew emotions and clear thinking don't always go together. I would act with more honor than my opponents from that day forward.

"I will leave a promissory note at the bank under the name of the school tomorrow," I said, smiling at him. "Oh, and by the way," I said as we still shook hands, "see that Jaggers never comes in contact with Miss Honing, and I expect to hear of no further problems," I added.

"But of course," he replied, walking to the door and holding it for me.

As I walked to the bank, I understood the saying that money talks. Well, if it did, I was going to make it scream.

Chapter XXII

Just Like Her Mother

After her talk with Jaggers, Etta Jean came to a decision. If her mother not only willed her a fortune but a life as well, she would at least try on that life to see if it fit. She would learn all there was to her mother's dynasty and meld into it. If it didn't work and she couldn't fit the part, she could let it run the way she received it – on its own. But if she did fit the part, who could say how far she could go?

Etta Jean's first stop was the Dark and Beautiful factory, it being the family's biggest moneymaker. Felicia Mansfield, the company manager, greeted her and brought her to her office.

"So, Mrs. Newman, how can I help you today?" Felicia asked.

"First off, there's no need to be so formal. I'd like for us to become friends. Please, call me Etta Jean."

"That would be nice," Felicia smiled. "Well then, Etta Jean, how can I help you?"

"I want to learn everything about the company."

"Of course, we can look through the books and…"

"No, that's not what I mean," Etta Jean said. "I want to learn everything. Don't worry; I'm not looking to replace you. I want to know how to run everything in the building. What is the lowest level of worker you have?"

Felicia thought about it for a moment. "I guess that would be the manual laborer's jobs. You know, sweeping up, putting labels on the jars, packing boxes."

"That would be great," Etta Jean said. "I can start there and work my way up. I want to know how to do every job in the company."

Felicia smiled brightly. "You know, you're a lot like you mother, and I mean that as a compliment."

"We'll see," Etta Jean thought out loud. "We'll see."

* * * * * * * *

Etta Jean was used to hard work from her days at the boarding house, so working at Dark and Beautiful was a breeze. She not only worked hard, but she observed all that was going on around her.

In time, she learned the ingredients to all the products. She learned to grind them, cook them, and mix them in the right proportions. The other workers knew who she was, but in time accepted her as one of their own. They saw how hard she worked and how friendly she could be, and in time everyone liked and respected her.

All the time she worked and observed, she was thinking of ways to improve working conditions and company sales.

After months of working and learning, Etta Jean had an idea she wanted to run passed Felicia. They met in Felicia's office.

"I must admit, you're a good worker," Felicia complemented her.

"Thank you. And I must admit you run this factory very well," Etta Jean replied. "But I do have a few questions."

"What is that?" Felicia asked.

"Why do the workers have to work so hard?"

"Because we haven't been able to keep up with our orders. Dark and Beautiful has become well-known and in great demand. We could double our income if we doubled our output."

"Why don't we add more workers?" Etta Jean asked.

"That would be great." Felicia said. "But where would we put them?"

"I've been watching and thinking," Etta Jean said. "We don't need another factory; we just need more workers. We have the room."

"Where is there more room?" Felicia asked.

"We can move the tables where the labels are applied into the warehouse; this would also be close to where they can pack the crates for shipment. We can ship twice as often to keep the space available."

"That just might work," Felicia admitted.

"And I want to set up an incentive program. The more a worker knows, the more they will be paid. That way, if someone is not available, someone else can do that job. In time, everyone will know how to do every job. That will allow workers to take off now and then, and not have to work endlessly."

Felicia smiled. "You are your mother's child."

* * * * * * * *

Next, Etta Jean went to meet with Tom Dunsany at the lumber camp.

"I know I'm not strong enough to be a lumberjack or to work in the mill. But I'd like you to humor me and teach me everything there is to know about the lumber business," Etta Jean asked Dunsany.

"I'd be glad to," Tom responded. "What would you like to know?"

"Everything. I want to know everything there is to know."

Tom was more than willing to teach Etta Jean the lumber business. It would be difficult, but Etta Jean was so willing to learn.

For the next few months, she rose early and went to the lumber camp. She learned the do and don'ts of felling trees, and how they are delivered to be cut, stored, and shipped.

The men were impressed with her willingness to learn. At first, they thought of her as a nuisance, but in time as they saw how serious she was, she gained their respect and loyalty.

After a few months of observing, Etta Jean had a few opinions of her own. She and Tom met in his office.

"I have to admit, you run this operation in an unbelievably efficient manner. It is near flawless, and you should be commended," Etta Jean proclaimed.

Tom sat there smiling, reveling in his boss's appraisal.

"But I do have some suggestions," Etta Jean stated, to Tom's dismay. "When you chop down a tree, what happens then?"

Tom looked at her with a confused expression.

"I don't know what you mean," he said. "We cut down the tree, we bring it to the lumberyard, and we cut it into planks and then ship those planks all over the country."

"That's fine," Etta Jean said. "But what about my daughter and your children?"

Tom laughed. "I don't understand what you're saying."

"The space where the tree once stood, what is there now?" she asked.

"A stump, of course," he replied.

"How long do you think we can keep doing that before we run out of trees?"

Tom laughed, "We could do it for years."

"But can we do it for generations?" Etta Jean asked. "I want to give my daughter something when I'm gone; I want to leave something for my grandchildren. From now on, we will dig up the stumps and then plant seedlings."

"Do you know how costly that will be?" Tom said.

"Do you know how costly it will be for our children if we don't?"

Tom understood the logic behind what Etta Jean said, but it was a can he and so many others had been willing to kick down the road for the next generations to deal with. Inwardly, respect for Etta Jean welled up in Tom.

For the next few weeks, Etta Jean was a fixture in the background. She watched and learned. In time, she told her findings.

Again, she praised Tom. "I'd like to say that you do an excellent job. You run everything like a fine ship. I know why my mother put you in charge. No one could do better," Etta Jean said.

"Well, that's kind of you to say that," Tom said with a smile.

"I do have one thought," Etta Jean added. "There seemed to be an awful lot of sawdust left over."

"That's a lumberyard for you," Tom replied.

"What do you do with the sawdust?" Etta Jean asked.

"We save some of it for the winter; we put it down on the roads leading to the saw mill. The ice makes it tough going; the sawdust give us traction. Also, the city uses some of it on the streets in the winter for the same reason."

"And what percentage is that?" Etta Jean asked.

"I'd say about a month's worth; the rest we disregard."

"I see," Etta Jean said. "I think I have a good idea what to do with the rest. Put aside the sawdust over the next few days for me."

Tom thought this a strange request, but was glad to do it.

* * * * * * * *

The next morning, Etta Jean had Morgan bring the flatbed wagon around to the front of the house, and then the two of them rode into town. Their first stop was Smith's Dry Goods.

"Good to see you, again, Mrs. Newman," Mrs. Smith said, rushing to her as soon as she entered. "Hans, come here; it's Mrs. Walker's daughter, Mrs. Newman," Mrs. Smith called to her husband who was stocking shelves in the back of the store.

"Please, call me Etta Jean, Mrs. Smith."

"Then you call us Hans and Maggie, *ja*? Now, how can I help you?"

"I'd like to buy thirty-five pounds of paraffin."

"Paraffin...wax...you make candles?" asked Maggie.

"Something like that," Etta Jean replied. "My driver and wagon are outside."

"Hans, go help Etta Jean with her order."

Next, they rode to the saw mill where Etta Jean asked for a barrel of sawdust. Tom watched as two of his men loaded the barrel onto the wagon.

"You mind me asking what you need all that sawdust for?" he asked Etta Jean.

"I've got an idea. We may just have us a new business."

Tom smiled and went back into the mill, shaking his head. "Just like her mother."

Etta Jean and Morgan drove to the Dark and Beautiful factory. Felicia greeted them.

"I've got an idea, and I need your help," Etta Jean said. "I want to put this wax over one of furnaces and melt it down. While it's still hot and liquid, I want to put it in a large mixing bowl. There we'll mix the hot wax with the sawdust, then take the mixture and pour it out on one of the tables, spreading it real good. Before it gets too hard, we need to cut it into small squares, say, two inches by two inches."

Felicia gave Etta Jean a questioning look.

"I'll explain as we go along," Etta Jean assured her. She turned to Morgan, "Ride back into town and ask Jaggers to come here."

Morgan was off in a wink. Felicia gave orders to start the process.

Later when Jaggers arrived, the concoction had firmed to small, square, grainy chunks.

"What do we have here?" Jaggers asked, examining the tiny bricks.

"This is our new endeavor," Etta Jean answered. "And as my lawyer, I'm putting you in charge of getting our first customer."

"What is this stuff?" Jaggers inquired, picking up one of the squares.

"It's a mixture of paraffin wax and sawdust," Etta Jean said, picking up her own square to examine and show. "Put a lit match to this and it will catch fire and burn under any condition. I don't care if it's high winds, rain, or snow, it will burn and cause whatever wood you pile around it to catch fire. That includes wet wood as well."

"I've heard of people using this," Jaggers commented, "but I've never heard of producing it to sell. So, who's our first costumer?"

"The United States Army," Etta Jean laughed. "I want you to go to the capital and sell this to the military. It's the perfect fire starter under any conditions. No soldier's pack should be without it."

"You know, it just might work," Jaggers laughed along with Etta Jean.

"Might I make a suggestion?" Felicia added. "It should be wrapped in paper, which is easy to catch fire. That would set the cube afire easier."

"That's a great idea," Etta Jean said, smiling at Felicia. "You just earned yourself ten percent of the profits." She looked to Morgan. "Morgan, ride downtown and bring back a roll of butcher paper." She looked to the others. "We'll wrap them in butcher paper – what a great idea." And without a word, Morgan was out the door.

A few hours later, after wrapping the cubes in butcher paper, they packed the samples in a box for Jaggers to take with him.

"So when do you want me to leave?" Jaggers asked Etta Jean.

"How about tomorrow, how does that sound?"

"Sounds just fine," Jaggers said. "Let's go into Felicia's office and write down what each of these cubes cost and what we can sell them for."

"There's one small issue," Felicia said. "You need a name. What are you going to call the product?"

They all thought for a moment.

Etta Jean looked to Morgan, who always had a clear way of looking at things. "So, Morgan, what should we call them?"

"Well, they're for starting fires, so I think you should call them Fire Starters."

"That can be part of it," Etta Jean said. "But we still need a company name."

Morgan smiled. "I got it. Name it after your daughter, Liberty...Liberty Fire Starters."

Everyone smiled and nodded their heads in agreement.

Etta Jean handed the box of samples to Jaggers. "There you go...the first batch of Liberty Fire Starters."

* * * * * * * *

In the middle of a field, Jaggers was surrounded by military brass and couple of senators. They'd made the test as hard as possible. The wood was damp and so was the ground. Winter was approaching, so there was frost on the ground, and the wind was blowing hard. The wood was piled in the manner soldiers in the field were taught to make a campfire. Above him hung a large washtub that had small holes in it to simulate a rainstorm. All it all, he was given poor and difficult conditions to start a fire, which was just what Jaggers hoped for.

With one lit match covered by Jaggers' hand, touching the edge of the paper wrapper around the cube, the paper caught fire, and in no time, the Liberty Fire Starter caught fire. It seemed to burn no matter what the conditions. In time, the small flame dried the wood, and it, too, caught fire till, despite everything against it, Jaggers had a full campfire.

Either the observers of the test showed little interest in order to get the price down, or they truly weren't interested. One of the senators picked up a sample, and then so did the others.

"You do know this is nothing new?" the senator said with an air of sarcasm. The others chuckled without trying to hide their finding it all humorous.

"Then why doesn't each soldier have something like this in his knapsack?" Jaggers asked, trying to sound innocent and friendly, though he wanted to attack them verbally and forcibly.

"These things cost money. We have priorities. Some things are more important," replied one of the generals.

"Tell that to a wet and freezing soldier in the field," Jaggers said, keeping his friendly tone. "Let me tell you our deal," Jaggers continued. "Each of you admits this is a good idea. It's just a question of cost. What if I could offer you our product at an affordable cost to you?"

They all stood silent, waiting for the next shoe to drop. Jaggers had done his homework well, and knew what the cost of production was and what was needed to make a profit. The cost was kept down because the sawdust was not only free, it didn't need to be shipped but a few miles down the road. The wax would cost less if they ordered it in larger quantity. They were close to the railway, so deliveries would not be difficult or so costly.

"I'll tell you what," Jaggers said. "We can offer you a price of one cent per cube with every order of five thousand. An order of ten thousand or more would bring the price down to half a cent."

"Does that include delivery?" asked the other senator.

"Yes, it does," Jaggers replied with pride.

Now they seemed interested.

"We will let you know," said the senator.

* * * * * * * *

It was a long and nervous wait for a reply from the government. In a leap of faith, Etta Jean not only ordered large quantities of paraffin wax, but hired three new workers to solely make the cubes at the factory. She had them make and store ten thousand cubes. After three months of no word from the government, Etta Jean still believed in the product. She ordered another ten thousand cubes to be made and stored.

Almost six months to the day, Jaggers visited Etta Jean at her home. He entered her office, waving the letter in his hand.

"Our first order...forty thousand!" Jaggers shouted, laughing as he danced across the room.

Etta Jean let out a long sigh and began to laugh also.

"And when word gets out the government is using Liberty Fire Starters, every general store and dry goods store in the country will want to carry it."

Jaggers took Etta Jean's hand, bowed, and kissed it. "My dear, you are a genius."

Chapter XXIII

Josephine and Helena

Each day, the hours and minutes dragged by, but the years flew by. The business took up much of my time. I kept receiving a bill each month from Morel in New York. Each time, there was no word of finding my children. I suppose anyone else would have given up, but I never gave up hope. I did receive a letter one year; Morel wrote that his agency wasn't having much luck. He advised that I either give up or he could put the case on the backburner and charge me less. I immediately replied that I didn't want to hear of such a thing. He was to continue at top priority, and I would continue to pay for priority service. The loss of my children tortured me. There was not an hour of every day that I didn't think and sulk over it.

Jaggers grew, and he grew fast and tall. I gave him all the time, support, and love I could. But the year his voice changed, it fell a full octave lower; I realized he needed to learn from men, to be around men. So I made arrangement with Tom at the saw mill that Jaggers would work each day after school and on Saturdays. It was hard work, and at first he couldn't understand why I put him through such misery. If we were rich, why did he need to work, especially a manual labor job? But in time, I believe he understood and eventually enjoyed the work, at least the comradery.

Perhaps it was his name that his father gave him, that inspired him to be like the Jaggers in the book and study law. I was pleased and encouraged him. When he became of age, we began looking into the better law schools in the country.

Of course, Jaggers' first choice was Harvard. But there was a problem. The school had closed during the Civil War, and they weren't able to secure any teachers in the legal department when they opened again after the war. And they had no idea when they would be able to move ahead with law studies again.

Jaggers' next choice was The Dickinson School of Law in Carlisle, Pennsylvania. We made some enquiries about the school. Of course, we could afford it. But there was another problem. The requirements for entry were numerous and intense. The student needed to have a background in classical language and literature, moral philosophy and religion, ancient and modern history, algebra, geometry, and calculus. They also would prefer some knowledge of constitutional law, mechanics, chemistry, optics, electricity, and magnetism.

Jaggers was a good student and had graduated with honors, but this was far too advanced for him. To his dismay, I advised him to wait another year and prepare himself. I would hire a tutor for the year, and knowing his abilities, I was sure he'd be ready the following year.

Not knowing where to start, I wrote a letter to Principal Tallmadge Russell from Jaggers' alma mater, where he recently graduated.

I've learned that when you expect something, be prepared for the unexpected. I was in my office when I was told there was a woman wanting to see me about the tutor's position. As you must assume if you believe time changes everything, the woman who came to see me was Miss Honing.

She was the same scrawny, hatchet-faced woman I remembered. My first inward reaction was a hostile one, but I decided to remain calm and listen.

"I must say, I'm surprise to see you," I told her.

"And I'm surprised to be here," she said. "I've come to apply for the tutoring job."

I told her, "I see. I know your qualifications, but there are other matters that need discussing."

"I realize that," she said. Then she went into a long silence with her head bowed and her hands shaking. Then she burst into tears.

I had her sit and poured her a glass of water. She drank it slowly. She wiped her eyes with her handkerchief. In time, she calmed down and was able to speak.

"I want to ask your forgiveness. Even if you don't accept my services, I'd like you to forgive me. So much has happened since we last met. I understand how wrong I was, and I'm sorry."

I had to ask her what brought about the about-face. Her answer surprised me.

"It was the hand of God," she said. I was taken aback. "I've told this to some people I know, most of them told me it was just a dream, but it wasn't. I woke up one morning and everything about me felt the same. I looked in the mirror and I was the same person I'd always been. But leaving my home, the world saw me different. Strangers and people I knew saw and treated me differently. Everyone spoke down to me. There were places I wasn't allowed to go. I lost my job. Stores and restaurants wouldn't serve me; even my church wouldn't have me. And everyone I asked would say, 'You're not one of us.' This went on for weeks, till finally I gave up. I came to accept my fate, but it was a sad day for me.

"Then out of nowhere, an angel appeared and said, 'Do you understand now?' And I said I did. The next day, I woke up and everything returned to the way it once was, back to normal. I was grateful, but ashamed of the way I once thought and lived. That's why I'm here today to ask your forgiveness and to give me the chance to show you how I've changed."

She went quiet. I thought perhaps she was the most impressive liar I'd ever met in my life, or she truly had an epiphany. I decided to accept her apology and hired her on the spot. After that, it was up to Jaggers to give her another chance. For the first few weeks, he was nervous around Miss Honing, sitting on pins and needles and walking on eggshells. But in time, they got along just fine. And in less than a year, Miss Honing felt Jaggers was ready to apply for The Dickinson School of Law. He did, and a letter arrived a few weeks later that he was accepted, and he could enroll and start in the fall.

It was a proud but bittersweet day we saw Jaggers off at the station. But most important to me, at least, was before he and I had our long and tearful goodbye, he gave Miss Honing a farewell hug.

****

We all missed Jaggers, but none like I did. I wrote him often but never expressed how much I missed him. I didn't want him to look back and feel obligated in anyway but to move forward with his life.

A year went by, and he was healthy and happy according to his letters, and his studies were going well. Fall was ending and winter was closing in. We anticipated a visit from Jaggers during the Christmas break.

It was in the month of November, a month before his visit, that I received a letter from Jaggers and a surprise that floored me.

Dearest Mother,

Let me start by telling you how much I love and respect you. I am not just writing this because it is true, but because I don't want you to think that I've gone around you in disrespect, nor have I tried to hide anything from you. This is just as much as a surprise to me as it is to you. It all seemed to happen so quickly.

There is no easy way to say this, so I will be straight forward. I have fallen in love, and I am now married. Her name is Josephine. She is a wonderful woman, and I'm sure you will like and approve of her. We plan to visit during the holiday break. I will forward all the details, as I learn them, in a following letter.

Know that I am the happiest I've ever been in my life. And I do know this is the right thing for Josephine and me. As you can imagine, there is much more to the story than a letter can hold. We will talk in December.

Again, I ask you to be understanding. I love you. Your loving son,

Jaggers

I was filled with mixed feelings. Of course, I was happy for Jaggers. But his letter left me with more questions than answers. One question being – God forgive me for thinking this way – but who and what was Josephine? Jaggers came from a mixed union; did Josephine know his background? Either way, all cards would be laid on the table in December.

* * * * * * * *

The weeks passed. I never had the nerve to write Jaggers with my questions, and neither did his letters suggest any answers. All I knew was the date and the train they would arrive on.

I spent my days preparing for their arrival. I stocked up on all Jaggers' favorite foods. I had the house covered in Christmas decorations, and I had the large guestroom prepared for their coming with flower arrangements placed wherever possible.

Finally, the day of their arrival came. Morgan and I set off for downtown with the larger buggy and one of the workers with a wagon for their luggage. I waited at the station platform, nervously staring down the tracks that stretched out into the horizon.

When the train pulled into the station, my heart was in my throat. When I saw Jaggers hop off the train onto the platform, our eyes met and he smiled at me. He turned to help his bride from the train. At first, all I saw was a slender arm with a delicate hand at the end of it. The long feminine fingers were covered by a black leather glove. She stepped down onto the platform.

Josephine was a beautiful, young white woman. She stood only up to Jaggers' chest. She was delicate in appearance with a waist that could fill Jaggers' one hand and no more. Her hair was raven-black, and her skin was whiter than Jaggers', whiter than any cloud. From that distance, she looked like a porcelain doll.

Jaggers pointed me out to her. She smiled and waved. As they approached, I was aware of her elegance. And if a person can make a good first impression, Josephine certainly did. She reached out with both hands to take mine, leaned forward, and kissed my check.

She addressed me with so much respect. "So nice to finally meet you, Mrs. Walker. Jaggers told me so much about you."

"Call me Elizabeth," I insisted. "And Jaggers told me very little about you. But something tells me it is going to be a pleasure finding out who you are," I said smiling, and I reached forward and hugged the child.

The ride home was pleasant with friendly small talk. We arrived in time for dinner. The kitchen kept everything warm, giving the couple time to settle into their room.

143

I'd invited Duncan for dinner, not only because he was a close family friend, but I wanted him to be a part of all this. Not only for his advice, but I wanted to observe his reaction to such matters.

The conversation around the dinner table was casual and jovial, but eventually turned to the matter on everyone's mind.

Her name was Josephine Madden, the daughter of Peter and Helena Madden. Mr. Madden was one of Jaggers' professors. The couple met at a party the Maddens held at their home, for students and faculty alike. It was a case of love at first sight. The two began seeing each other socially immediately, and in time began their courtship. The Maddens liked Jaggers from the start, and he was a guest for many dinner parties in their home.

To Peter and Helena Madden, the problem wasn't their approval of Jaggers; it was the speed the young couple rushed into their plans. Within a few months, the two lovers were talking marriage. This was the cause of many an argument in the Madden home. In time, rather than cause a rift between Josephine and her parents, Jaggers backed away and agreed to a much longer engagement. But as the holidays approached, everyone's plans changed.

"We were married only last week," Jaggers admitted with a smile.

"Last week?" I questioned, sounding suspicious. "So your parents relented? Let me guess; you're having a baby," I said, looking at them both.

"Yes, isn't it wonderful?" Josephine said, gleefully taking hold of Jaggers' hand.

As they looked happily into each other's eyes, they didn't see me shaking my head. You're never more impulsive than when you're young.

"You were married last week, you're with child, and now you're here. I don't understand."

"Let me explain," Jaggers said. "Josephine's parents went along on one condition; that they could tell family and friends we were to go on an extended honeymoon in Europe for a year."

"But you'll stay here to have the baby, wait a few months, and then return to school," I said, finishing up.

"Yes," Jaggers said, "we didn't think you'd mind."

"Now, I have a few questions," I said, first looking to Josephine. "Has Jaggers told you about his parents and who I am?" I asked her straight out.

Still holding Jaggers' hand, she said softly, "Yes, I know, and it doesn't matter."

"I'm glad you feel that way," I said. "Now, tell me what you've told your parents."

This time, she was slow to answer. "They don't know any of what we've spoken of," she replied.

"What did you tell them about me?" I asked Jaggers.

"You're my aunt, that's all, and that we'll be staying here till after the baby comes," he said.

"I guess it's my fault," I said to Jaggers. "I taught you not to pay mind to what color a person is, and I guess now you don't see it at all."

They both looked at me with a questioning expression.

"You do understand," I said, "that there's no way you can know what color this baby is going to be? What would your parents do if you have a black baby?" I directed this question to Josephine. A sad look came upon her. "And you," I said, pointing at Jaggers. "How will you make a living and where with a white wife and a black baby?" Then I turned to Duncan. "And what have you got to say about this, sitting there all quiet?"

"What is your problem?" he shouted at me across the table. "They're young and in love. And of course they're going to have problems – all people have problems. True, their problems will be unique, but if they love each other, they'll get through it." He was shaking his head at me. "I don't understand you with all these questions. I've always known you as an independent black woman, and I've looked up to you for that. But now you're acting like all the people you've despised. I don't understand."

I began crying; I knew he was right.

"I'm sorry," I said. "I'm so...scared."

Sweet Josephine reached out and placed her hand on mine. "It's all right. We all get scared sometimes."

"I'm a good midwife, you know?" I said through the tears.

"I wouldn't have anyone else," Josephine said, squeezing my hand.

* * * * * * * *

Josephine was concerned about Jaggers' education. To wait till the baby was born, and then wait months till he returned to school would slow his pursuit of graduating to a slow crawl. She wrote her parents, suggesting that Jaggers return early from their so-called honeymoon to start in the curriculum the first part of the year. They could tell family and friends that Josephine continued to tour Europe without Jaggers. They could announce her pregnancy months later. After all, it only takes one night, as Josephine and Jaggers learned the hard way. Then she would return with their child to be with her husband.

Logically, it made the best sense. Josephine would be in good hands and Jaggers would not have to postpone his studies. But there was a drawback. Jaggers would miss the birth of his child. This bothered him, but on the insistence of his wife, he conceded to follow the plan.

Many tears and kisses were shed and exchanged the day Jaggers left to return to school. Josephine promised to write him every day and I swore to wire him any important news and changes as soon as I knew them.

As the weeks slowly crawled by, Josephine began to show. She remained skinny, but clearly with child. Josephine and I became close friends and I can honestly say I loved her. This only made me all the more ashamed of myself. Here I was loving and caring for my daughter-in-law, and there were my children somewhere out there not benefiting from my good fortune.

As the date approached, we made arrangements. We set up the guestroom where Josephine slept. We did artificial run-throughs, rehearsals, so when the time came everything would go smoothly.

When the day came, we thought we were ready, but we weren't, not for what surprised us. At first, everything seemed to be normal and was going smoothly. But then it turned bad. It just wasn't happening the way it should, and I didn't know what to do. I ordered Morgan to rush and get the doctor, but it was too late. He had no idea what do to beside hope and pray, which we had been doing for hours.

Just after midnight, the doctor came from the room. He wore the longest and sadist of faces. Before he spoke, I knew what he had to say wasn't going to be good.

"We lost them both, mother and child. She was so small, and the baby was large and in a strange position. We were helpless. I did what I could, but it was out of my hands. Whatever you do, don't blame yourself. No one could have changed what happened tonight."

I held my hand to the wall to stop from falling to the floor in a faint.

"It was a girl," he said softly," and it was..."

"Don't tell me," I shouted fast enough to stop him. "I just want to know if it was a boy or a girl. That's important. I don't want know if it was black or white, because that doesn't matter. If I were to ask you, then I would make it important, and it's not. All I know is my daughter-in-law has died, along with my niece. And that's all that matters."

****

One of the hardest things in my life was the wire I sent to Jaggers. He was on a train and home in just a few days. Josephine's parents came with him. Awkwardly, we met, they stayed with us, and they paid their respects to the two graves in the family cemetery behind the house. They'd named the baby Helena, after Josephine's mother.

We spoke little, and besides being shocked at the sight of me, not a word about race ever was raised. They stayed three days and were on the east-bound train on the morning of the fourth.

As for Jaggers, he was crushed. There are points in each life, both good and bad, that define your life. I had taught Jaggers to continue even during the storms of life, but he would never be the same. That sorrow would remain a part of him. The names of his wife and child would resonate in him with each heartbeat, and like a scar deep in the soul, he would carry the sadness for the rest of his life.

Chapter XXIV

Uncle Willy

Jaggers entered Etta Jean's office wearing a smile. "I've got some good news," he said, taking a seat in front of Etta Jean's desk.

"Before that," Etta Jean said, "I read what Momma wrote about you and Josephine. And I'm sorry."

The smile turned to a look of thoughtfulness. "Thank you. Well, you know, it was a long time ago."

"If you ever need to talk about it, I'm here," she announced.

They fell silent for a moment.

"I have a question for you," Etta Jean said. "I've read so much about Duncan. Were they really sweet on each other, Momma and him? And whatever happened to him?"

The smile returned to Jaggers' face. "Well, they were close, but I don't think anything ever became of it, at least I don't think it did. You'll have to keep reading to find out. As for Duncan, he was a miner in these parts, got very rich, and one day sold it all, left, and no one's heard of him since."

Etta Jean grew thoughtful for a moment. She felt a strong urge to excuse herself and go upstairs and continue reading her mother's diary. Perhaps the answer was further on in the pages?

Jaggers' smile grew even bigger, as he held up a letter. "Don't you want to hear the good news?" He waved the sheet of paper even higher. "It's from Detective Paul Morel. They found one of your brothers, your brother Willy, or in my case, my brother, or Cousin Willy. Maybe I'll call him Uncle."

A look of shock came over Etta Jean. "Willy was the oldest. I don't know much about him. Where is he?"

"He still lives in the South, in Alabama, in Montgomery. He's married and has six children, all grown now. He works in a foundry. Morel sent the address."

Etta Jean hesitated for a long time, thinking. "Pack your things. You and I are going to visit Uncle Willy."

* * * * * * *

Etta Jean and Jaggers traveled swiftly by train, first class all the way. Of course, this turned a few heads and caused a few stares. Not wanting any trouble, whenever they needed to stay in a town for more than a day, they stayed at a hotel in the black part of town and ate only at black restaurants.

Even so, they still received stares and jeers. Thankfully, every clerk at every hotel was a gossiping big mouth. Word was out that they slept in separate rooms. This eased the tension. In the years after the war, you needed to be careful; it left everyone touchy and definitely scared. But most frightening of all, the war left many people, both black and white, angry. And a friendly face many times hid someone with evil intent. After the war, the South was overrun with wolves in sheep's clothing.

They arrived in Montgomery late at night. They got two rooms at the better of the two hotels in the black part of town, which had a small restaurant on the first floor, where they ate. After questioning the locals, it became evident that getting around in the poorer part of town and locating someone would be difficult. Many of the small shacks didn't have a number and were on dirt roads that bore no name. They decided that in the morning they'd visit the one black church for miles. If Uncle Willy was a churchgoing man, they might find out where he lived.

With the morning light, they walked down to The Good Shepherd Church. The Reverend Malcolm Rosewater was a friendly old soul with a near toothless grin and as many wrinkles in his black face as a map of the Mississippi River and its tributaries.

"Willy Walker...sure, I know him. Poor man's been through enough misery lately to make the story of Job sound like the vaudeville. Two years ago, his son, Rupert, came down with the fever. Died in less than a week. Then he lost his job when the foundry closed down after the war. He's been working picking crops, here and there. He couldn't afford to keep his place, so he moved to the poorest part of town. It's just an old shack like so many others, just one room and a stove. Then if that don't beat all, last year his wife, Celina, died of what nobody knows. He's been living in the same shack with his daughter, Adela. That poor child, she ain't nothing but a child of twelve, but she takes care of that house just like her momma. She looks ten years older than she be. They come to church only on holidays, as poor Willy has gotta work every day to get by. I can take ya to them, if ya like," Reverend Rosewater concluded. Etta Jean and Jaggers took him up on his offer.

They followed Reverend Rosewater to the edge of town, through areas that didn't even have a proper road. When they came to a row of one-room shacks, Reverend

Rosewater stepped onto the porch of one and knocked on the door. A lanky, young black girl came to the door. After talking for a minute, they were invited in.

"Daddy will be home very soon. Please find a place to sit," Adela said apologetically.

It was obvious they were poor. In the one room, there were two cots, a table with four chairs, and a few shelves that held a bag of flour and one of coffee over an oven. There was a pot of greens boiling slowly.

A half hour later, in walked Willy. He looked tired and worn, his head balding and his skin cracking from working twelve hours a day in the sun.

"Reverend Rosewater?" he said, and looked at the others. "What's this about?"

"These people have come a long ways to speak with you," the reverend replied. "I think it would be best if I let them tell you."

Etta Jean rose up and stood in front of Willy. "Willy, my name is Etta Jean Newman. I used to be Etta Jean Walker...I'm your sister."

"That can't be. Etta Jean died when she was just a baby," he argued.

"No, that was Emma May, my twin sister. I'm Etta Jean. Don't you remember?"

Willy sat down and stared at her.

"Our momma was named Elizabeth, and Daddy's name was Richard. We also had a brother named Henry. When all of us were little, we were all sold away from one another. Momma's been looking for all of us for years. I hate to tell you this, but our mother is dead. I've continued the search for our family, and now I've found you."

Willy pointed to the empty chair in front of him.

"Mrs. Newman, please sit down."

Etta Jean thought this strange, but sat down anyway.

"Mrs. Newman, I'm not your brother, Willy." He looked towards Reverend Rosewater. "In fact, I'm not Willy Walker. My real name is Jeffery Stoner." He again turned to Etta Jean. "I knew your brother – Willy. He was a good friend of mine. We were slaves on the Whittle Plantation here in south Alabama.

"It was a terrible place. They treated their slaves bad. Few lived longer than five years. Willy and I used to talk about our pasts to each other. That's how I knew about your sister, Emma May. I guess I forgot you was twins. He also mentioned a brother named Henry. He told me he was dead. He never told me how he died.

"Anyways, I guess the plantation owner fell on hard times like all the other plantations during the war. Many of the weaker slaves were going to be auctioned off. Your brother was one of those slaves. In fact, he so weak and sickly that he died the night before the auction people was to come and collect them.

"God forgive me, but I just had to get out of there. I saw no harm in it. After all, your brother was beyond suffering. So I switched clothes with him and name tags, too. They used to make us wear name tags.

"The next day, in all the confusion, I got lost in the shuffle. As far as they were concerned, they buried Jeffery Stoner and sold Willy Walker. I lived and worked the next few years at a different plantation. Not a nice place, but far better than the Whittle place. After the war, the plantation fell into ruins, and all the slaves were freed. I came to Montgomery looking for work, and I've been here ever since. I was afraid to go back to my old name, so I stayed being Willy Walker.

"So you see, Mrs. Walker, I'm not your Willy. I wish I was. I'd like to have a family, and you seem like a nice lady. Please, forgive me."

"There's nothing to be forgiven for," Etta Jean said. "We all did what we had to do to survive."

Everyone stood up. Etta Jean and Mr. Stoner shook hands. Then Etta Jean went over to Adela and shook her hand, too.

"God bless you both," Reverend Rosewater said as they left the shack and started their walk back to the church.

When they'd gone, Adela was crying.

"What's the matter, sweetheart?" Mr. Stoner asked his daughter.

"Look what that lady just snuck into my hand when we shook hands."

The child held up a coin – it was a one-hundred-dollar gold piece.

Chapter XXV

Two Great Losses

Months later, after the death of Josephine, everything returned to normal, at least in appearances. Jaggers returned to school, though he left with a broken heart. He wrote me to tell me that the Maddens, Josephine's parents, stayed close to him. And not wanting to make a stir, they never mentioned his background to anyone, or the woman he called mother.

As for me, I continued to work and prosper. I kept in communication with Paul Morel, always hoping for good news. I always hoped to see my children again.

It was at this time in my life that I decided to speak openly with Duncan. So many years passed, and our friendship grew closer. And in all those years, I never forgot Christina's words, "He's sweet on you." My mind never forgot it or wanted to admit it, but my heart wanted so desperately for it to be true. I never met a man I liked as much as Duncan or wanted one as much as him. The day came when I knew I had to tell him how I felt. The way he spoke that day when Josephine and Jaggers told their story made me hopeful. But still there was no way to tell which way the wind was blowing.

I sent word inviting Duncan to the house for dinner. This was not an uncommon practice, and he sent word he would. I gave the staff the day off, and spent the entire day in the kitchen preparing his favorite dishes.

In the evening when he arrived, we had brandies and talked for some time about what was going on in our lives and the area — small talk. In the dining room, I sat at the head of the table with him close at my right. The table was already covered with platters and bowls of food. It took some time before he realized there were no workers around and that we were alone.

The small talk continued throughout dinner. Knowing what I was about to do filled me with fear. I didn't want to lose him; I wanted him to continue in my life. But looking at him in the glow of candlelight and listening to his voice, so close to me, I knew I couldn't live another day without him knowing how I felt. Nor could I go on not knowing what he felt for me.

Later in the parlor, again over brandy, we sat and talked. Outside, darkness had fallen, and with only a fire in the fireplace to light us, we were cozy and warm.

"So what is this all about?" he asked.

"What's what about?" I replied, trying to sound coy. "I've had you over for dinner hundreds of times."

"Yeah, but you made all my favorite dishes. There's nobody else in sight; the room is as dark as a half-moon night. And you're all dolled up like a princess in a fairytale," he said, trying not to sound too serious.

"We need to talk," I said, sounding very serious. "We've known each other a long time now. And for a long time, there's been an undercurrent flowing between us that I think it's about time we talked about it." I said this very straight forward. I only hoped I didn't sound too businesslike and cold. But I had to start the conversation, and to me this was the only way.

Duncan sat motionless and silent for the longest time, but you could see behind his eyes, his mind was racing. Finally, he looked at me with those soft eyes of his welling up with tears.

"I love you," he whispered, sitting far from me. "I don't know when I started to love you, but I don't remember a time when I didn't. So many times I've stood near you, trembling inside. Whenever we touched, later I'd put my hands to my face just to take in the scent of you. I can't tell you how often I wanted to reach out and kiss you."

"What stopped you?" I asked him.

"Mostly I was afraid you'd say, 'No,'" he said.

I told him, "What if I told you I felt the same?"

He stood, walked to me, took my hand, and pulled me up into his arms. We kissed; it was heavenly – so soft were his lips.

Just as quickly, he stopped kissing me and backed away from me.

"That wasn't the only reason I never told you how I felt," he said. A fear came over me, as I knew there was only one real reason he felt he couldn't love me. At that moment, I knew our love affair was over before it ever started, and my heart was breaking.

"I'm a hypocrite," he said out loud. "I attacked you when you hounded Jaggers and Josephine. I said that all that mattered was that they loved each other. But now that the shoe is on the other foot…" He turned from me, as if afraid to look at me. "I know what I'm saying is wrong and selfish, but I can't seem to stop feeling this way. I fear a life with a black woman. I think of my business, my status, and my reputation. I know how wrong this is, but I can't make myself be something I'm not.

"Oh, I could easily carry you upstairs to your room, here, tonight, in the dark of night. But tomorrow, in the light of day, to claim you as mine to the world…"

He turned to look at me. I was shaking and crying so hard that he and the world were a blur.

"Do you hate me?" he whispered.

I sighed deeply. "No, I don't hate you."

He reached out for me. His touch burned me like a fire.

"Please, don't touch me," I pleaded.

He let go and backed away. I could hardly see through the tears. A moment later, I realized he'd left the room. When I heard the front door close behind him, I fell to the floor, weeping.

****

For some days, Duncan and I had no contact. I suppose we both needed time to heal. In that time, I was visited by an interesting stranger.

His name was Calvin Adams, a young, handsome black man and so well-dressed. He was a professor from Bowie State University in Maryland. He'd come all the way across country to speak with me, but he was the bearer of sad tidings.

He asked for an interview, which I granted immediately. He was in the middle of writing a book on the black heroes of the Civil War. He'd been traveling the country collecting information on these heroes, one of which was my son, Henry.

I had not seen or heard a word about my son since the day we were sold and scattered. To learn that he was a hero during the war filled me with pride. But my joy was short lived when I learned he was long dead.

Mr. Adams planned to dedicate an entire chapter to Henry and came to learn what he could from his mother. It was interesting that Paul Morel, well-paid Paul Morel, couldn't find anything on Henry, and here this East Coast professor knows the whole story.

I was unable to help him; I knew so little of my son. It was all a surprise to me. Mr. Adams told me Henry's story in detail. He left disappointed but very thankful. A year later, he was kind enough to send me a copy of his book, appropriately titled: Black Heroes of the Civil War.

****

Weeks passed. I thought it was time to reach out to Duncan. If anything, we were still friends, and I didn't want to lose that. I sent a letter to his house. It was heartfelt, explaining that no matter what, I still wanted him in my life. I never received a reply. Finally, in frustration I rode downtown to his office. To my surprise, it was vacant. I didn't know what to do so I went to the bank where he did all of his business.

I was in for the shock of my life. I learned that Duncan had sold everything he owned in the world to the bank. They were willing to take it all off his hands; he'd given them such a ridiculously low price, they couldn't refuse. They planned to make a killing.

When I asked if they knew where he'd gone to, they had no idea. Usually, funds that large are transferred by wire to another bank. But he'd demanded payment in cash, a foolish thing to do, but it didn't leave a trail.

I was frantic. I knew it was a waste of time, but I rode out to his home. There was a "For Sale" sign outside the house and all the doors and windows were boarded up. I stood on the porch and peeked between the slats of wood and through the window. The house was dark, but there was enough light coming in to see that there was nothing left, not even dust.

From there I rode up into the hills to one of his mines. I was met with the same story. Everything was owned by the bank and up for sale. The price was so low that they expected to be bought out by a conglomerate within the month.

As I was about to leave, I caught sight of Old Gus. He was a tall and slender old white man who'd started mining in his youth, but never hit a strike. But his knowledge made him valuable, so he worked on the mines of others. Duncan had known him for years and made him a manager of one of his mines. Gus was a salty old prospector, a bit uncouth at times and always needing a shave, but no one knew mining as well or had a bigger smile or a kinder heart.

"Gus…Gus!" I shouted till I got his attention. He walked over to my buggy.

"Mrs. Newman, what y'all doin' up around here?" he asked.

I told him, "I've learned about Duncan selling everything. What do you know about it? Do you know where he is?"

"I probably don't know much more about it than you do," he replied. "Duncan was looking poorly and acting mighty strange the past month or so. I asked him what was wrong, but he'd never say.

"Finally, one day he takes me aside and tells me he sold everything and he was leavin'. I told him he was crazy. And ya know what he said? He said, 'Yeah, I know.' Ain't that a hoot?"

"So you don't know where he's gone to?" I asked, trying to hold back the tears.

"Naw, he wouldn't say. Crazy, ain't it? But he did finally tell me why he was leavin'."

"He did?" I asked. "Why did he leave?" I just had to know.

Gus' words went through me like a hot knife.

"He told me it was because of a woman. Crazy thing…he didn't tell me who she was, but she must have been something to get him to act that a way. Crazy, ain't it?"

Chapter XXVI

Uncle Henry

Early in the morning, before anyone else was awake, after a night of reading her mother's journal, Etta Jean went downstairs to the library. She ran her finger across the books on the shelves, scanning the titles. She found it on one of the first shelves, in the middle, like a place of honor. She read the title.

Black Heroes of the Civil War
By
Calvin Adams

She took the book down, found a comfortable seat by a window for the morning light, and began to thumb through it. It was a thick book covered in leather with fine gold page edges, looking almost like a Bible. Reading the list of contents, there were many chapters, each titled for the hero it spoke about. It didn't take her long to find the chapter about her brother. It was a quick read, but it kept her mesmerized and took her breath away.

Chapter Seventeen
Henry Walker

Since slavery hit the shores of the Americas, there was a strong debate for and against it within the white community. Understandably, these white sympathizers lived mostly in the North, but not all. These like-minded broke up into two groups: those who struggled to have the laws changed, and those who felt talk was useless and cheap, and went the way of the sword. They felt violence was justified in their cause.

Of the latter, the most famous was John Brown, whom we mentioned in the second chapter. Depending on your view, some say he did much good and movements like his are some of the reasons that pushed the country into war. Brown didn't live long enough to even know of the Civil

War. He was captured and hung some three years before war was declared. Many were inspired by his methods.

One of the many white abolitionists who attacked slavery in the same manner was Cedric Butler. He was a New Yorker who settled in the South and formed a small band of like-minded white men to fight against slavery wherever they found it.

Butler's band of warriors did not remain small for long. Many of those opposing slavery, usually young, white men – students mostly -- joined Butler's Brigade, as they were called. But what increased the brigade's number were the young slaves whom the brigade freed in raids on farms and plantations. These young men were usually those without families or ties, willing to give their life, if need be, for the cause.

Butler came to a point where he needed to make a decision. Either let the brigade's number increase till they were an army to themselves, or break up into smaller units acting separately and attacking different parts of the South. His decision was the latter, feeling small groups would do the most good.

One of the leaders of these offshoot groups was a former slave named Henry Walker. There is not much known about Henry Walker other than he was freed from a plantation by Butler's Brigade and formed his own movement of twenty other former slaves who would attack small farms and free other slaves.

I visited Henry's mother, Elizabeth Walker, an entrepreneur living in Colorado. Sadly, she had little to say concerning her son, as they were separated during the war, sold at a slave auction to different masters, which was the case with so many families at the time.

Little else is known of Henry Walker and his men other than they went roving about the countryside for three years. Their basic strategy was to hit a farm or even a small Confederate troop late at night, do as much damage as they could in as short a time as possible and then retreat. They hid in the woods, living on natural sources and whatever supplies they got from fallen soldiers. It was a well-known fact that Henry Walker and his men were in contact with Union Troops and often worked in cooperation with them. This was to be their downfall.

A troop of Union soldiers were en route to a high plateau in southern Virginia near Chesapeake. Their orders were to take and hold their ground there. A troop of Confederates were on their way to stop them. Their only obstacle was the waters of Deep Creek, a tributary of the Elizabeth River. The Confederates marched to the slimmest part of the river, hoping to cross. Henry Walker anticipated this, and he and his men met them at that point. Though vastly outnumbered, Walker and his men held off the Confederates for forty-eight hours, giving the Union Troops more than enough time to secure their objective.

Sadly, Henry Walker and his men were defeated and killed. There is little record of this encounter, and there is not even a plaque to commemorate the efforts and passing of so many brave men.

Etta Jean slowly closed the book and placed it back on the shelf in its place of honor.

Chapter XXVII

All I Have to Give

Time moved slowly and sweetly. Jaggers completed his studies with honors. When he returned home, he was puzzled about what way his life should go. Good lawyers were needed everywhere, and adventure calls to a young man. His first thoughts were of moving to San Francisco, the booming city on the bay. He went out to inspect it, but decided it was not for him. He'd been on the east coast for so long; he knew for certain that part of the world wasn't for him. The South was still recovering from the war; it was a good time for lawyers and politicians. But he thought the weather not to his liking.

It didn't take me long to realize Jaggers was happiest in Denver. Understand, he wasn't a momma's boy; it wasn't just me he would be missing. He'd been raised in Colorado, and no place else on earth felt as much like home.

"Why don't you set up an office in town?" I told him. "I could use a personal lawyer, someone to oversee my business matters."

This was probably the worst thing I could have said to him. He took it as me babying him, saying he couldn't make it on his own. He was ready to take the next train leaving Denver going to anywhere.

It took me weeks of insisting that my intent was not to coddle him. "No, I'm serious," I told him. "I really could use the help, and who better than someone I trust?"

He finally gave in and was willing to give it a try. We set him up with an office downtown on the second floor of one of the newer buildings. He insisted that such things were nothing but a loan, and he would pay me back in time.

"Why would you do that?" I asked him. "When I'm dead and gone, you'll get everything I own anyways."

But he went on, insisting he needed to pay me back. In a way, I was glad. It made me believe I raised him right.

In time, it became evident we'd both made the right decision. Jaggers' talents were just what the business needed. Our efficiency increased, and in turn, so did our profits. Everyone liked and respected Jaggers, which made things easier. As well, I never saw him so happy. It was as if he were made for the job. In his spare time, he took up practicing law for others in the town, small affairs like deeds and wills. In time, the entire city respected him and sought out his talents. But he spent most of his time seeing to the family business, and soon that was all he did.

There were times he would travel to meetings across the country. It was not my intention, but these meetings went smother when business men were confronted by a young, handsome, intelligent white man, instead of an aging black woman such as me. Heck, they hated doing business with women in general, and when I showed up, everything turned sour fast. But with Jaggers doing these meetings, business transactions went smoother, faster, and more profitable.

Still, as happy as we all were, I had one strong concern for Jaggers. After the death of Josephine and his child, that part of him became numb. There was not one young woman in the city of Denver that could turn his head. I talked to him about the matter, but he had little to say about it, only that he wasn't interested and if lightning were to strike in the same place twice, then so be it. But until it did, he wasn't interested.

****

Life ain't easy. Even when it's the best it can be it ain't easy. And you never know which way it will go. Don't ever be fooled that when things are bad, it can't get much worse, 'cause it can, just as much as it can get better. As well, don't ever forget that when things are good, they can get better. But most folks, when all is going well, are thrown for a loop when things go bad, and sometimes they do.

It came on me so slowly. I didn't realize what was happening until it was too late. It started with the unshakable feeling of being tired. But who hasn't experienced such things in their life, especially if your days are filled with hours of work? You know what it's like. You wake up tired, and you can't shake it off. You think if you only had a day off, you could catch up. And when that doesn't work, you tell yourself one day just won't be enough. You wait for it to pass, but it doesn't, and in time it gets worse. Yet, it becomes familiar, a part of your life, and you ignore and accept it.

Then, in time, others around you begin to take notice. They ask if you're feeling well. They comment that you've lost weight. They look at your plate and ask if that is all you are going to eat.

Your reply is always the same: you feel just fine; you suppose you've lost a few pounds, and that you're just not that hungry. If you say it enough times, you start to believe it yourself.

The next appearance within this affliction is a cough. Nothing odd or out of place; everyone coughs. Perhaps it's a bit harsher and more frequent, but just a cough. Then it becomes noticeable; the coughing slowly becomes harder, deeper, and more often. So you take some time off and it lessens, but only for the time you rest. Once you are on the go again, it is right back where you left it.

The next phase is dramatic, but still not enough to take caution. You wake in the morning and you have phlegm. Nothing unusual at first, just morning phlegm. But one morning, it's thicker and larger than usual. You still don't take caution.

But then one day, there is blood in what you coughed up. There is something about blood that catches your attention. The connection of blood to life is without question. It is only then no excuses can be made. Foolishly, with your tail tucked between your legs, you go see the doctor.

They try to make little of it. They tell you just stay home and rest, plenty of rest, and you will heal. But they tell you this to give you hope, which is in small supply.

So you follow the doctor's orders. You stay in bed; you rest and take care. But the coughing becomes worse; the speckles of blood are now splotches that stain the sheets. And one day, you find the strength to get out of bed and walk to the mirror. You look, and you see someone that bears no resemblance to you. It is time to think differently; it is time to prepare to die.

So you prepare yourself. You get your affairs in order and you wait for the consumption to consume. And just when you think there is nothing else to contend with other than the Grim Reaper, you get a letter.

Dear Elizabeth,

It's been a long time; I hope this letter finds you well. I can hardly contain my excitement; I have such good news. We have located one of your children, Etta Jean.

At first, we weren't sure. All the documentation seemed in order, but you know how that goes. Things aren't always what they seem. So I sent one of my men to check it out. I am happy to say our suspicions were confirmed. I can safely say this woman is your daughter Etta Jean.

I might add that at no time during our investigation did we contact your daughter, nor does she know of our investigation. Which brings me to the topic of contacting her. Of course, I leave that decision up to you.

Let me state the different options. I can have one of our men contact her face-to-face, and explain the circumstances in detail. Or we can have one of our lawyers in her area do so. As well, since the situation is an emotional one, some of our clientele have asked for a clergyman to do the first contact.

Another alternative is we post a letter to your daughter explaining what has happened. I do not recommend this; as I mentioned, it is a delicate matter. We usually reserve this method for legal matters only.

And finally, you or someone you trust will make the first contact. Just let me know what you've decided.

The details of our investigation, as well as your daughter's location, are on the attached paperwork.

I wait for your instructions. Again, I hope this letter finds you well.

Yours in waiting,

Paul Morel

It was truly bittersweet news. I was happy to learn that my Etta Jean was alive. The sorrow I felt when I learned about Henry was erased by such wonderful news. I thanked God over and over. To learn that she was alive and well, it was a dream come true. And reading the report, I learned of her sorrows, that she was a widow and working in a boarding house. But best of all, I had a granddaughter as well. I cried with joy for such blessings.

But I also cried tears of sorrow. I knew I would never meet either one of them in this world; I would have to wait to see them in the next. Still, I wanted so badly to connect somehow, even in death. This is why I have written this journal, for you, my child, Etta Jean, and my granddaughter, Liberty.

I spoke with Jaggers, the one person I can trust to do what I ask and follow through. We talked it over and decided that all I own and am will go to you, Etta Jean, save for a large bank account I put aside for Jaggers. He's to spring this on you slowly, in phases, if he can.

To some my dynasty may seem like so much to give to someone. But I know it's nothing compared to what can flow between a mother and daughter. I am so sorry, but it's all I have to give.

How do you say goodbye to someone you've never really met?

Chapter XXVIII

Meet on the Ledge

We used to say that come the day
We'd all be making songs
Or finding better words
These ideas never lasted long

The way is up along the road
The air is growing thin
Too many friends who tried
Blown off this mountain by the wind

Meet on the ledge, we're gonna meet on the ledge
When my time is up I'm gonna see all my friends
Meet on the ledge, we're gonna meet on the ledge
If you really mean it, it all comes round again

— Richard Thompson

The morning light poured into Etta Jean's bedroom like honey, slow and golden. She woke, sitting in her chair, her mother's journal in her lap. It was still open to the last page. She gently closed it and held it to her chest, her arms tightly wrapped around it.

She couldn't explain what had happened to her. Something had changed in her and in the world. All her life she had felt motherless, a sad way to feel. But now that feeling was gone. She had a mother, she knew her name, and she knew that she was loved by her. And isn't that all a child could hope for?

She placed the book on the table before her, rubbing her hand across the cover with affection. She left her room and tiptoed into Liberty's room.

163

It was still early and the child was fast asleep. Etta Jean looked upon her sleeping daughter and tears welled in her eyes. She couldn't resist the urge to reach out and touch the child ever so gently, and then she bent low and kissed Liberty on the forehead.

As she stood up, the child's eyes opened and a smile came to her face like a flower in bloom.

"Momma…?"

"I'm sorry I woke you, darling," Etta Jean said as she sat down on the edge of the bed and began stroking Liberty's hair back, which the child always liked.

There was a questioning look on Liberty's face.

"Liberty, are you happy here?"

Still smiling, the child nodded.

"Do you feel safe?"

Again, Liberty nodded.

"Do I make you feel loved?"

Liberty sat up and wrapped her arms around her mother's neck. "Oh, Momma, I do, and I love you, too."

That was all Etta Jean needed to hear.

"Get washed and dressed, and I'll meet you downstairs for breakfast," Etta Jean said as she kissed Liberty on the forehead again, rose from the bed, and left the room.

Etta Jean went downstairs and entered the kitchen; there she found Morgan.

"Morgan, please do me a favor," she said. "Go fetch Jaggers. Ask him to please come here today."

Morgan nodded and headed for the door.

"Oh, and tell him to bring four large bouquets of flowers," Etta Jean told him.

He thought this an odd request, but he just nodded. "Yessum," he answered as he left.

Etta Jean and Liberty sat alone at the dining table, eating their breakfast.

"I've sent word to your school that you won't be attending today," Etta Jean said.

Liberty's face lit up with a pleasant surprise.

"I have something to ask you," Etta Jean said. Liberty sat up and looked astutely towards her mother. "When Auntie Faye died and you went to her grave at the small cemetery down the road, did you see any other graves?"

"There was one that Jaggers took me to. He told me it was where my grandmother is buried. I didn't know I had a grandmother," Liberty spoke in a childish and inquisitive tone.

"Yes, you did. She was my mother. I never told you about her because I never knew her."

"You never knew your mother?" the child asked, sounding surprise at a statement that sounded so unreal to her.

"Not really. We were separated when I was very young, younger than you are now. I lived with people, good people, but not family people. I was on my own at a very early age, till I met your daddy. I'm sorry I spoke little about him to you. I miss him so much, talking about him hurts, but that was unfair to you. If you ever want to talk about him or ask questions, don't be afraid to come to me."

"Was he a nice man?" Liberty asked

"Oh, yes, darling, he was one of the nicest men you'd ever meet."

"And did you love him?"

"More that you can imagine."

"And Grandma, did you love her?"

Etta Jean took a long moment to answer. "That's why you need to learn all you can about someone. You can't love what you don't know, and the more you know, the more you love. So, I guess you can say I love Grandma."

"What was Grandma like?"

"Well, she must have been pretty, because you're pretty." This statement confused Liberty some, but it made her smile. Etta Jean continued, "She was a smart woman and a hard worker. But best of all, she refused to let anything or anyone stop her from succeeding: not hatred, not prejudice, not being a woman, and definitely not skin color."

Just then, Jaggers entered the dining room, carrying four large and beautiful bouquets of flowers.

"Will these do?" he asked, holding up the bouquets.

"Why, yes, they're lovely," Etta Jean responded.

"What's this all about?" he asked. "What, did somebody die?"

To his surprise, Etta Jean smiled at him and said, "Yes." Then she turned to her daughter and took her hand. "And it's about time I went and paid my respects."

***

Though it was a short walk to the family cemetery behind the house, Jaggers insisted they take the carriage, and he was to drive it. He extended his hand to help Liberty and then Etta Jean into the buggy. It was all done with great protocol and fanfare. Etta Jean held two bouquets and Liberty held the other two. Jaggers drove the buggy slowly, emphasizing the importance of the moment.

When they arrived at the cemetery, Jaggers jumped down and again offered his hand to help them down from the buggy. The small plot of land was surrounded by a hip-high metal fence. Jaggers held the gate opened for them to enter.

Etta Jean handed two of the bouquets to Jaggers. He didn't need to be told what they were for. He placed one on his wife's grave and the other on his daughter's. He smiled a thank you at Etta Jean for being so thoughtful.

Liberty rushed to Faye's grave and placed the flowers on it. Etta Jean watched, feeling such loss and how much she missed her dear friend. She felt ashamed that she hadn't paid her respects till now.

Then they moved to her mother's grave. The headstone was tall and gray. Etta Jean stood before it in tears. She placed the flowers down on the grave.

She felt Jaggers and Liberty close to her. She reached out and took hold of both their hands, Jaggers to her left and Liberty to her right. Through the tears, she looked at the tombstone of her mother and read the epitaph:

Elizabeth Walker

Loving friend and mother
Gone to be with her Lord
December 10, 1885

Born a colored girl
Lived and died
A Black Woman

The End

Michael Edwin Q. is available for book interviews and personal appearances. For more information contact:

Michael Edwin Q.
C/O Advantage Books
P.O. Box 160847
Altamonte Springs, FL 32716
michaeledwinq.com

To purchase additional copies of this book visit our bookstore website at:
www.advbookstore.com

Longwood, Florida, USA
"we bring dreams to life" ™
www.advbookstore.com

CPSIA information can be obtained
at www.ICGtesting.com
Printed in the USA
FFOW01n2103100618
47075691-49481FF

9 781597 554787